LETTER FROM A GREAT-UNCLE

By Richard Hall

THE BUTTERSCOTCH PRINCE
COUPLINGS, A BOOK OF STORIES
LETTER FROM A GREAT-UNCLE & OTHER STORIES
THREE PLAYS FOR A GAY THEATER

Letter from a Great-Uncle & Other Stories

by
Richard Hall

Grey Fox Press
San Francisco

Manufactured in the United States of America.

Library of Congress cataloging in publication data

Hall, Richard Walter, 1926—
    Letter from a great-uncle & other stories.

    Contents: Letter from a great-uncle — The purple prince—
The night visitors — [etc.]
    1. Homosexuality, Male—Fiction.   I. Title.
PS3558.A3735L48   1985   813'.54   84-15798
ISBN 0-912516-88-7 (pbk.)

Distributed by the Subterranean Company, P.O. Box 10234, Eugene, OR 97440.

For
Byrne Foyne

CONTENTS

Author's Note

The stories in this collection, only two of which have been previously published, need little introduction. They came out of many times, moods, places; whatever merit they possess cannot be increased by a description of my reasons for writing them.

However, the title story, "Letter from a Great-Uncle," deserves a note on its sources. The tale is based partly on the life of my own great-uncle. Like Harris Belansky in the story, he was born to Polish immigrant parents in Texas just after the Civil War, was homosexual, and had to leave home because of a sex scandal. He settled in New York City and lived there all his adult life, working at Stern Brothers, a department store on 23rd Street, eventually rising to a managerial position. He was an avid theatergoer and died at the Hotel Langwell, just off Times Square, in 1936, when I was ten. I have many memories of him from his visits to our home in White Plains and was especially aware of a bond between us. Even at an early age I knew, in some unfathomable way, that we had deep things in common.

Because of this bond, or heritage, I have long wanted to reconstruct my great-uncle's life, trying to imagine the crucial events that forced him into exile from Texas. In attempting this I have drawn on certain family traditions and records, including his own father's participation in the Civil War and later founding of a dry-goods store. I have also used public documents of the time, and have relied on the research of certain social/sexual historians, including Havelock Ellis and Martin Duberman. I am especially indebted to Jonathan Katz, whose two pioneer works, *Gay American History* (1976) and *Gay/Lesbian Almanac* (1983), gave me valuable clues to the period, and who was kind enough to read my manuscript and make helpful suggestions for change.

The photo on the cover of this book is of my great-uncle and was taken, I believe, for his high-school graduation. It is reproduced here with permission of the Austin-Travis County Collection, Austin Public Library.

LETTER FROM A GREAT-UNCLE

Letter from a Great-Uncle

The letter was a family tradition. It existed but no one knew where. When discovered it would shed light on certain mysteries—why Uncle Harris spent time in the famous state asylum in Gideon, what scandal lay behind his exile from Texas, why he passed his life up north among Yankees.

He was actually my mother's uncle, my own great-uncle. He was an old man when I knew him—tall, spare, blue-eyed, with a head like a polished knob. He carried an amber-headed cane, wore spats and a pince-nez. He spoke in an elegant wheeze that had almost erased his Texas accent—fifty years in New York City had left their mark. He was, in short, a dandy.

He often visited our home in White Plains, a suburb of the city, for Sunday dinner. He came chiefly to see his sister, my grandmother, who lived with us. He was also fond of my mother. To my father, who despised him, he was cool and polite. But of course I remember most clearly his attentions to me.

He would often make me sit beside him and tell him about my school, friends, games, stamp collection. (He too was a collector, of theater programs; he had attended first-nights on Broadway all his life.) Of course, I loved this. Grown-ups tended to focus on my older sister, a dazzling creature who would do one of her specialty dances at the slightest provocation. But Uncle Harris preferred my company. He would tell me little stories about his own childhood, which I listened to eagerly, looking for clues that might help me get through my own. Once, shortly before his death, he promised to tell me the whole story when I was older. I instantly demanded to hear it all, at once.

He died in 1936, at the age of 72, in the cluttered room of the Hotel Langwell near Times Square where he had lived for almost half a century. I was very upset when I heard the news. I remember quite clearly that I said to my best friend, "Uncle Harris was the only one who ever loved me." I now believe that this statement, absurd on the face of it, reflects a deeper truth. Although I was only ten at the time of his death, I knew in some unfathomable way that we had important things in common. He understood me in a way that no one else did; hence his "love" was more valuable than that of other, less perceptive relations.

Over the years my memory of Uncle Harris faded. I had my own life to live, after all. Occasionally I would think about his collection of theatrical programs, probably quite valuable, and the famous letter. I decided that these must have been among his personal effects acquired by some cousins in El Paso. I made no effort to trace them.

But not long after reaching my fiftieth birthday, I found myself thinking about Uncle Harris again. Certain remarks, uttered more than forty years before, rose from a jumble of memories. "They used to call him Miss Priss at home." "There was a terrible scandal and he had to leave Texas." "Daddy hated him, he was an awful sissie." I made inquiries. Yes, Uncle Harris had been homosexual. It must run in the family. Nobody knew what had happened back in Gideon, it was too long ago.

And then, one evening as I was planning my annual trip to San Francisco, I remembered his old promise to tell me about his childhood. The promise had not been kept and now I was curious. Who was Uncle Harris? What kind of life had he led? The next morning I realized what I had to do. I had to go to Gideon and try to find out. I called my travel agent and arranged for a detour to Texas enroute to California. It seemed suddenly, as I hung up the phone, that this journey, this engagement, had been hanging over me for four decades.

After a great deal of telephoning, I discovered that the personal papers of Harris Belansky had been sent to the Gideon Public Library, where they comprised part of the Travis County collection of historical materials. I would be welcome to examine them. I allotted two days for this—surely enough to turn up whatever documents had survived.

I confess that my first reaction, on a stifling day in June, to the four cartons of material put at my disposal in a carrel in the public library in Gideon was one of dismay. Followed by intense boredom. It would take me a week to read through all this! My trip to San Francisco, with many pleasant diversions planned, would be delayed. Besides, the cartons contained heaps of material that had nothing to do with Uncle Harris—wedding and obituary notices, ledgers and licenses, business contracts, land sales, ladies' seminary reports, dance programs, all relating to other members of my mother's family. I really wasn't interested.

And then I discovered the photograph.

It was of a young man with clear blue eyes, a Cupid's-bow mouth, angelic hair and pointy ears. He was elegantly dressed in a high stiff collar, flowered cravat with a stickpin, jacket of heavy worsted with a yellow rose (for Texas) in his lapel. A high-school graduation picture, I thought, probably dating to 1882.

As I continued rummaging in the cartons, I propped the photo in front of me. From time to time I scanned it. Each time I found it more appealing. In the sweetness of the gaze, in the guilelessness of the tilted lips, I heard a faint plea, a subtle request: *Know me, hear me.* I had come a long way to do just that, I thought, but was not having much success.

By nightfall of the second day it was obvious that the famous letter wasn't here. It had probably never existed, I thought, piling everything back into the cartons. Except for the photo, which I planned to have copied, I had discovered nothing of interest. It was when I was standing up, stretching, that the sticker on the outside of one carton caught my eye. *Donated by Mrs. Minna Frees, 1974.* The name rang a bell—a cousin who lived in Gideon and had sent Christmas cards until my mother's death. I had never met her. Was she still alive?

The curator informed me that Cousin Minna Frees was around 80 and partly blind. I called from the hotel that evening. The voice on the other end was faint and querulous. My name meant nothing but when I mentioned my mother, there was a long pause and then the voice grew shrill. "I remember you when you were a little boy! Will you come and see me?" After a moment's hesitation—it would mean postponing my departure—I said I would, next morning.

Minna Frees lived in the new section of town—handsome brick homes, two-car garages, buried lawn sprinklers, swimming pools. A Mexican maid opened the door, then ushered me into the living room. A small woman was sitting forward in a wing chair. Her eyes were large, black, unfocused. When I went to her she pulled me down. "Kissin' cousins," she breathed. Her skin was dry and cold. It struck me that her spirit was stronger than her body — that, perhaps, she was in charge of a corpse.

As we talked I realized she was no ordinary widow. She had traveled widely, sat on bank and charity boards, supported all the arts and raised three distinguished children. As she spoke of these things, and I spoke of myself, I had the feeling that she could see me quite clearly despite her defects of sight. A moment later I wondered if I had merely succumbed to the delusion of all homecomings: that we are known in our blood, our flesh, our prehistory, which may substitute for more particular matters.

At any rate, after the maid had brought in coffee, Cousin Minna settled back and said, "Now tell me what brings you back to Gideon."

As I spoke of Uncle Harris, and my curiosity about him, she kept her dark eyes on me. I had the feeling she was hearing much more than I cared to say. Finally, stumbling slightly, I came to the letter. For some reason I found myself deprecating it. "There was this story — my mother always used to talk about a letter. I think she did it to tease us." I laughed nervously. "Nobody really believed her."

"Oh my." Her voice was light and high. "I thought everybody had forgotten all about that letter."

My throat was suddenly dry. "You mean there is a letter?"

"Of course."

"Well . . . why didn't she get a copy of it?"

Cousin Minna gave a harsh laugh. "Your mother? The Yankee branch of the family? Why should they? They all hated Gideon."

It was true. My mother detested her origins. It suddenly struck me that her flight to the north in the 1920s had duplicated that of Uncle Harris, earlier than her own by forty years. I wondered if the relatives who remained, like Cousin Minna, considered this a betrayal.

"May I ask . . ." I was having trouble controlling my voice, ". . .where the letter is now?"

Her black eyes searched my face. Again I had the impression she could read me clearly. She lifted a shuddery hand to her face as if to wipe away cobwebs. "You know my mother Jennie was Uncle Harris' favorite sister." She paused. I wondered if I was being tested in some way. Did I have to prove myself loyal? Worthy? And then none of that mattered because she picked up the bell on the table at her side and rang. "Since you came all this way," she murmured.

The maid returned. "Alicia, please show our guest to the library."

She turned her dark gaze toward me. "You will find an album on the bottom shelf of the bookcase. In it an envelope, addressed to Jennie, marked Private."

She reached into the crevice of her chair and brought up some tinted glasses. Behind them, she looked frail, diminished. "I will wait for you here," she said.

She waved aside my stammered thanks as if they too were cobwebs. I followed Alicia into the library, standing around while she turned on the air conditioner. When I was alone I searched the bookcases — there were four. The album was buried beneath some huge editions of Milton and Dante with illustrations by Gustave Doré. The envelope, thick and brown, lay sandwiched between two heavy cardboard pages, each mounted with photos of Uncle Harris as a boy. I recognized the innocent gaze, the pointy ears, the Cupid's-bow mouth. But to my surprise, the envelope was sealed with red wax. The seal looked very old. I wondered why it was still unbroken.

It might sound odd but I sat for a long time before opening the envelope. Now that the moment was here, I was filled with anxiety. Suppose the letter was trivial or evasive? Suppose it was full of lies or self-justification? Then there was the question of privacy. Even though I was curious, something in me recoiled from hearing confessions — especially those to which I had not been invited. But then, as I was sitting there paralyzed, an old conversation echoed in my memory. In White Plains, a lifetime ago, Uncle Harris had promised to tell me his story when I was older. Well, I was certainly old enough now. Perhaps I had the right, after all.

With a deep breath, in anticipation of pain, I broke the red seal. The sheaf of papers inside was embossed with the gothic tower and the legend of the Hotel Langwell. The first page was dated November 26, 1936, and was addressed to Jennie. I began to read.

I am writing this at a time when I imagine all of you are sitting down to the Thanksgiving Feast. I will be alone although I have had several invitations. Both Mr. Hubbell from the store and Josephine Sims, Asa's spinster sister in Staten Island, have asked me. But Dr. Burwell says I am not to exert myself so far. I will sit here by the window looking out on 44th Street and write to you, Sister. The city is quiet because of the Feast and I will have peace to think. I prefer that to traveling about nowadays.

My thoughts have been going back to Mamma and Papa. It gives me pleasure to recall. I often regret that you and I did not talk frankly in the old days. This will have to stand for the conversations we never had, at least aloud. We will remember together, at last.

Over the past few months (you know we had a very warm autumn here, the warmest they say since '18), I have sat long hours by my window thinking. Yes, I have sat here, the odors of the city thick in my nostrils—the ordure of the remaining horses, the rubbage of the restaurant next door, the stench of the thousands who bathe but once a week—and thought about home. For once, I do not feel like jabbering with my friends and neighbors, though they are kind. I was always able to jabber a blue streak, as you know, but that is finished now. I am content.

Last night Mamma appeared to me in a dream. She wore her long dress with the cherry bows and on her head a bit of lace. You know I was the one who persuaded Papa to carry lace. I said people are going to want lace tablecloths, lace trimmings to their sleeves, lace for their hats, so let's buy some. At first he refused but I won out in the end. To my sorrow.

Anyway, Mamma looked beautiful in the dream, a fine lady, quite the Governor's wife (Mrs. Hogg herself) and she looked at me sweetly with her blue eyes and said, "Harris, don't tell lies." And I replied, "Mamma, you always wanted me to lie to you, why should I stop now?" And then she dabbed her eye with a hankie and disappeared.

That dream stayed with me all through breakfast today, which consisted of oatmeal and Postum at the doctor's order (two foul concoctions) and I said to myself, maybe Mamma came back for a reason. Maybe she wants me to write down the truth about everything. I thought about this all day and have come to the conclusion that the dream was a sign. A sign that I am not to be snatched out of this world before I tell the truth.

Before beginning, let me remind you that I have had to live my life among strangers. I have become a Yankee. I think like a Yankee, I speak like a Yankee and for aught I know I look like one too. It was very difficult when I arrived. I found New York City a mean and hateful place, full of foreigners. The picture I had of it, the picture drawn up by the drummers and merchants who called on us at the store, did not turn out to be true. I missed home in those days. I thought I could not survive here.

But now I know that the events that led me here were my salvation. Yes, my salvation, strange as that sounds. I learned how to live here, to live my own life as God has given it to me despite the fact that so doing meant the loss of old friends and family. Here I learned how to be myself, amid the ill will and animosity, among the vehicular snarls, the corruption and the babble of foreign tongues. I often felt the ache of the homeless, true, and even thought of myself as an immigrant more tempest-tossed than those just arrived, but in time that gave way to jubilation. The jubilation of the free. By unshackling the chains of family I was able to forge a life of my own. By losing my place in the smaller world I found my place in the larger. Now I believe I would not have missed my life for anything, not even for the chance to stay home and raise a family. As I said, I am content. I discovered that the way down and the way up are one path.

Now that is said, I can go on with my story. I have much to tell and will tell it with what art I can muster.

As you know, Papa and Mamma came from Poland (although that part of it, Posen, was owned by the Prussians in those days). Why, after landing in New Orleans, they chose Texas I cannot understand. It hadn't been part of the Union for more than a dozen years. It was full of brawlers and desperadoes—a regular elysium of rogues. Papa might have opened his dry-goods store in New Orleans to greater advantage. There were dozens of dressmakers there who had learned their needle skills in Paris, there were Creole ladies who went to fancy balls every night. But no, he wanted to push west. And if Papa made up his mind about something, that was that.

When I first went to work in the store, and we were having such trouble getting our goods up the Colorado (they came on little flat-bottom boats then, before the railroad was completed), I asked him why he hadn't chosen Houston or Galveston instead of Gideon. There were cotton and cattle fortunes in those towns—money everywhere. I didn't get much of an answer, just that grunt of his. What did we have in Gideon? Mostly poor folk and lawyers hanging around the courthouse looking for business. Still, there we were and nothing to be done.

As you know, I was begotten during the intermission between the battles of Chickamauga and Atlanta—September, 1863, and May, 1864, on one of Papa's furloughs from the Texas Brigade. It was another stroke of his bad luck that he rode with Hood, that ill-starred general who never lost a skirmish nor won a battle. I don't think Papa cared much that he was twice cited for bravery. It was something he had to do and he did it. I believe that even had he heard the funeral citation, passed as a resolution of respect by the John B. Hood Camp of the Confederate Veterans on his death in 1911 at the age of 86, he wouldn't have cared. *A soldier brave and true and loyal to his adopted country, the southland.* No, he probably would have grunted into his beard and asked Mamma to pass the potatoes.

I came along in December 1864, the last of the brood and the only boy. I do not need to review all the faults that stemmed from that. Sometimes I thought I had four mothers, one by birthing and three by sistering, and every last one as sweet to me as sugared pecans. If, by some mischance, I didn't get what I wanted, I screamed and held my breath. When any sister saw me turning red she fetched what I pleased. I thought of myself as half-boy, half-hoptoad. I have since concluded that children are mostly imaginary beings, at least to themselves.

And now let me confess a second fault. Not only was I willful, I was a vain little creature. Although I thought all my sisters beautiful — Hannah tall and elegant, Lillie stout and babyfaced, you Jennie, petite and demure — I knew that I was more beautiful still. In a family whose looks ran to sallow skin and bistre-brown eyes, I was a glowing child with cornsilk hair and dimples. I was petted, paraded, indulged. I monopolized Mamma's lap. No wonder Papa had so much trouble with me later on.

Do you remember the night you were all dressing for the San Jacinto Ball? I was ten or eleven; the year must have been 1875. I was furious because I wasn't going with you. I wanted to wear the same outfits you did — dresses of coral velvet trimmed with swan's down, crystal beads around my neck. When you all laughed, I tried my red-in-the-face trick. This time it didn't work. So, just before you were ready to leave, I threw face talc all over your skirts. It was not a pretty thing to do. Papa gave me the worst hiding I ever had — I couldn't sit down for an hour.

Another occasion comes to mind. You girls had invited some beaux over for a candy-pulling. I was not supposed to be present but I sneaked down and hid behind the settee. When Lillie's boy went to kiss her I jumped out and pushed her head in the molasses. It took Mamma two days to get the mess out. But I didn't mind the punishment. It was worth it. You see, I was jealous.

But despite my shenanigans, I was a terrible crybaby. I was afraid of things—scorpions, snakes, the dark, thorns, rivers, even horses. I didn't learn to harness Beauty to the wagon until I was almost fifteen. Yes, vain, willful, mischievous, weepy as a willow. I was not the kind of boy that Papa deserved, although he never once expressed general disappointment with me. How sad that I didn't respect him then. Now I think of him as a hero. I am proud to be his son. It often happens too late, as those with sons and daughters discover, I reckon.

I won't review my schooling. But I still have my copy of *Enoch Arden*, though I've lost the essay for which it was the prize—"Why the South Should Have Won the War." I remember thinking I was a mighty handsome fellow when I walked to the podium to receive the prize book. Talk about a swelled head!

But I have skipped over some things and it is these I want to write about. These that Mamma, in my dream, requested. But I think I will wait until tomorrow for that. It is dark and my hand is cramped. Now that I am started, nothing—not even a poor night's rest—will keep me from finishing this.

It is the morrow, an overcast day with wind from the west. We will have rain, I think. I am not refreshed but will continue anyway.

My greatest pleasure, even when very small, was to watch the acrobats and riders when the Grand Continental Circus came to town. I loved the animals, the clowns, the midgets, but most of all I loved the swoops and somersaults, the daredevil deeds, of the athletes. People told me that circus actors were wicked and would steal little boys and I must never approach the tents alone. But that only served to excite my interest. I would hide where I could watch them walk around, so lithe and graceful in their fleshling tights, for the few weeks each year when they camped near the river.

There was one bareback rider, a sort of jockey, who thrilled me most. Sometimes I would wait all day for a sight of him, overcoming my fear and offering to carry water or spread sawdust. He noticed me once or twice and tried to speak, but he was a foreigner and we could not communicate. When I was asked at home where I'd been, I would say, "The circus," but I never told the truth. I never told anyone what drew me there.

I believe I knew even then that there was something different about me, that I was drawn by images and temptations the other boys did not have. But most of the time I was free in my mind. I liked the circus. Why should I reproach myself? I knew myself to be as healthy as milk.

But that was before Enzo appeared. To the best of my recollection, the Flying Fandangos joined the Grand Continental in 1879, when I was fifteen. Besides Enzo there was a sister and two younger brothers. Their family name was Fandarno—Sicilian. It had gotten hispanified into Fandango.

Enzo Fandarno summed up all that I found attractive in the male form. He was large and nobly proportioned, with a face of classic symmetry—broad forehead, brief straight nose, rounded cheeks. He had the sinewy musculature of all aerialists.

It wasn't long before we had a friendly acquaintance. I was of an age with one of his brothers and it was easy for him to take me under his wing. Sometimes he allowed me to hold the rope while he practiced. Other times, I would set up the ring-mounts for him. Afterward we would sit in the kitchen tent drinking sarsaparilla and he would tell me (in his poor English) about his travels, his *fidanzata* in Palermo, the dangers of his calling. He always spoke to me seriously. His conversation was never flash and cheap. During these talks I thought I was on a ladder leading to heaven.

Did you guess my inmost thoughts, Jennie? One evening at supper, while the other girls were gassing about their scrapbooks, you looked at me hard and asked why I was so quiet. It wasn't like me to be quiet, Lord knows. Then you asked, in that keen way of yours, if I had been to the circus that day. I was terrified Mamma would overhear—she had forbidden me to go there—but she was talking Polish with Papa. I pacified you somehow and changed the subject. Later, after all the trouble, I suppose you surmised where it started. But you never let on, for which I was grateful. You might have prized the truth out of me by trickery.

My chief weakness, I know now, was that I was extravagantly affectionate. There seemed to be something in my nature which demanded love and attention. This has been true all my life. At one time I believed it was the failing of certain men who resemble women in their dependency on individual love. Now I believe it is the property of the human race as a whole. At any event, at the age of fifteen I could only follow my natural instincts. I was about as civilized as a yellow dog.

I remember standing in the dust of Mission Street and watching the circus wagons rattle south toward San Antone when their season in Gideon ended. Enzo was driving a pair of grey Percherons. I cried and cried. I didn't want to lose him. I didn't want to live a whole year without him. I thought he was the most perfect being I had ever known, embodying the mysterious secret of masculine energy.

It is clear where I am headed in this letter. I am speaking of private matters. I am emboldened to this by the frankness with which they are treated now, not only in scientific journals (some of which I have read) but also in respectable books and magazines. In fact, the subject which once had only the most meager of names, is now introduced regularly into conversation. It has been a sorrow to me all my life that I never once spoke of these matters within the family, except when a doctor was present. It is now or never.

To continue. It wasn't long before thoughts of Enzo began to invade my reveries. I saw him at odd times—while running errands after school, sweeping the bare-dirt yard in front of the privy, lolling by the river waiting for the perch to bite. He always appeared in the same way—naked except for a breechclout which hid his majestic loins. Soon I improved on these reveries. I engaged in a solitary activity, usually at bedtime. The first time it happened I was startled at the result. Papa had never given me any education in this matter. But in time I became accustomed to it, especially after learning from my schoolmates that they had the same results.

Of course, I was always aware, without being told, of the danger of my habits. Such warnings seemed to be in the air at the time—practices such as this would interrupt my growth, damage my nervous system, prevent me from learning and ultimately lead me to a madhouse. Well, the latter turned out to be correct, but not for the reason given.

I remember that, on several evenings, Mamma looked at me oddly when I said I was going to bed. I was not in the habit of retiring before they threatened me with dire punishment. But here I was, on the stroke of eight, actually volunteering. After some weeks of this I saw her trade glances with Papa. I should have taken the hint.

And then it happened. Papa burst in and caught me in flagrante. Luckily, though he held the lamp high, he could not read the contents of my mind. Later, I shuddered at his reaction had he seen Enzo as clearly as I did at that moment!

He put down the lamp with his usual care. Then he took me by the throat so I could not cry out and flailed me methodically about the face and ears. He might have been whupping Beauty for pulling to the left. And he said nothing, not a word.

When he left me I rolled over and wept. But underneath, in my wounded pride, I planned my revenge. Willfulness and injured vanity would have their way, as they would for years to come.

Mamma was very quiet next morning, refusing even to look at me—at me, the apple of her eye! She put the grits and sausage and coffee on without even humming her morning song. I wish I could say I was ashamed, that I was burnt up with remorse. But I wasn't. I had made my plans.

Mr. Buckner at the livery stable knew me, of course, and swallowed my story about a delivery without thinking twice. By eight o'clock I was on my way, my schoolbooks dumped behind the Baptist Church, my chestnut mare with a white blaze loping smoothly across the prairie dotted with mesquite that lay between Gideon and the Guadalupe River. I figured I would put up in New Braunfels, where they knew us, and be in San Antone by sundown tomorrow. After that it would be easy to find the Grand Continental. There was only one circus in these parts.

I can still recall the mix of emotion—excitement, fear, willfulness, love—that filled me. Enzo would take care of me. I would become his son. I would never lay eyes on Mamma and Papa again. A new life would start.

At the same time I knew I had embarked on a career of vice. Running away would lead only to more trouble. Yet I couldn't stop, any more than I could stop breathing or dreaming.

My escapade ended quickly. Papa was waiting for me at the feed-store this side of Mason. Mr. Buckner had apprised him of my departure and he had lit out after me. Not on Beauty—she was too old and fat—but on a huge claybank I had never seen. Looking at Papa on that horse reminded me of how the Yankee soldiers must have seen him fifteen years earlier—a fierce and brutal man. Later I found out the claybank was Mr. Buckner's personal mount.

I reckon I was frightened going home—frightened by the silence, full of unslaked fury, that possessed Papa more than anything else. Still, I promised myself that I would run away again. And again, if need be. I would never stay at home. (That turned out to be true, but under very changed circumstances.)

The family was very subdued that night. I suppose my behavior exceeded anything that had happened before in that little saltbox of a house. But I kept my chin up. What else could I do?

The homeopath to whom Papa took me next morning was a new-comer. Dr. Santvoord. His office was on Tenth Street. He had come to Gideon to tend to the physical, as opposed to the mental, ailments of the maniacs at the state asylum. He also accepted patients privately.

Dr. Santvoord was a long, cadaverous man, almost as bony as the skeleton standing in a corner of his sanctum. He had a face like a knife and a grip of iron. He kept his large, dark eyes on me as Papa gave him details. I gazed downward. When Papa finished, Dr. Santvoord asked him to wait outside. Then, after lighting his pipe, he threatened me with terrible punishment if I continued my ways. Spermatorrhea, he said, would destroy everything from my posture to my growth to the marrow in my bones. I would become permanently debased, a walking corpse. By the time he finished the tears were rolling down my cheeks. He was a medical man, as old as Papa, with infinite knowledge. He was right and I was wrong—no doubt about it. Finally I raised up and looked him in the eye. He waited to hear me speak, give my promise. But some devil prevented me. Some devil of waywardness and mischief that all my life has kept me from submitting to the opinions of experts. It came in handy later but not at that time. So I wiped my eyes, kicked the rung of my chair and refused to speak.

Papa carried a parcel home with us. He set it on the seat of the buckboard. It was large and irregular. I didn't inquire, though I was sure it was connected to my refusal to promise. Papa looked too grim for questions.

Supper that night was a funeral. I tried some of my tricks, joking and larking as if nothing had happened, but nobody was fooled.

I have long since forgiven Papa for what he did that night. I believe he was acting from the best of motives, from his deep conviction, based on everything he knew, that he was helping me grow up to be a true man. If my thoughts were not pure, if I could not control the bestial part of my nature, I would be unfit for decent society. Eroto-mania, he believed (though he couldn't have known the word) would only lead me to an early grave. True love would never come my way. People's views have changed greatly since then, purity and chastity have been derided and sex-love has been praised. Nowadays it's con-sidered beneficial, and not necessarily in moderation. But remember that Papa was born in the early part of the last century and raised by parents born in the century before. Sometimes I think that overindulgence in practical matters narrowed him. But they were all like that in those days. At the zenith of our civilization people lived in the most rigid state of repression. Still, as I say, Papa thought he was doing right and I have long since forgiven him.

On the evening of which I speak, he ordered me to retire early. I had been in my room for almost an hour when he appeared. Not alone but with Sam, who loved us children so much. (Later that night I would curse Sam and believe that his childhood in slavery was as nothing to the torments of mine.) They had brought with them the contents of the mysterious package. I sat bolt upright, determined to fight whatever it was. But Papa had foreseen that. Without speaking they tied my hands and feet with belt-straps. After I was trussed like a turkey they produced the contraption.

It was an assemblage of canvas and buckles and brass loops. And something else. Even now the blood rises to my forehead as I think of it. I lay there, unable to move, my eyes swollen with weeping, as they strapped it on. It was of tent-canvas, heavy and coarse, and reached from waist to knee. Behind my back where I could not reach to undo it, it was tied and looped. When it was in place, Papa spoke. "You will wear this, Harris, until I give you permission to remove it. Every night, until I trust you." Or words to that effect. You know how hard he was to understand—but that night I understood clearly.

After they left I explored my canvas girdle. Its most shameful feature was a metal cup, in the center front. A slit had been made in the canvas and my parts had been passed through, into the cup. The designer, foreseeing everything, had placed a hinged flap at the tip of the cup, to be opened for bodily functioning. There was no way I could touch myself; I had been ingeniously thwarted.

After my exploration was complete I lay back and howled. I howled with shame and despair. With hatred and thwarted vanity. And before I fell asleep, almost choked on my own venom, I vowed that I would make them all pay. You cannot cross a willful boy too far.

I donned the canvas corset each night for the next several months. What was its effect? Almost nil. The rest of the day my hands were free. And I made use of them. But there was another, more pernicious result of which I wish to speak. The experience made a liar out of me, one of the smoothest in the state. Never again did I tell anyone in the family what I really thought or felt. Never again did I even say where

I was going, if a lie would do as well. Prevarications and evasions poured out of me. I mistrusted everyone and in time they came to mistrust me. My original sweetness was lost. It was the bitterest lesson of my growing up.

Another day has dawned and I feel a weariness that I fear nothing can relieve. Doctor Burwell has been here again—he is a kind man but too young to be trusted—and warned me again about exertion. I told him I sit all day by the window writing a letter. That seems to meet his approval.

I wish to speak now of my state of mind during those years.

Gradually, due to my smash on Enzo and others (and by the way, Enzo never returned, having married and set up house in his native land), I began to wonder if I was a female soul in a male body. Since I felt the erotic emotion of the "other sex" this was the logical conclusion to draw. Certainly I was vain and a crybaby.

Still, there were arguments on the other side. I wasn't fussy or peevish. I could drive a nail straight. I could whistle. There was no trace of gynecomasty. I was not languorous or weak-limbed. I had never fainted in my life. And I had had several proposals of marriage (half-joking to be sure) from older women before I was twenty.

Nor did I have any desire to dress as a woman. I wasn't drawn to any of those tortures—false hair, hoops, frizzes. Mostly I pitied women for having to dress in petticoats and underclothing, yards and yards of it.

So there is a picture of my confusion. I would often lie by the river, alone, and try to figure it out. I never could, but I was able to keep my deepest fears at bay. At least until I saw the Indian couple.

I was helping Papa at the new store every day after school—he had expanded to include foodstuffs and was very busy. They rode in on their pinto ponies, then stood on our gallery a long time conferring. I wouldn't have given them a second look—I was unpacking a shipment of corduroy braccas, just received—except for something peculiar about the squaw. She was the biggest I had ever seen—tall and broad-shouldered, with hands like wheelbarrows. She looked like she would burst her calico dress.

Just then Strap Cookson came in, took a gander at the squaw and muttered something about how nowadays you can't put an inch of knife into an Indian without getting into trouble. The Indian couple gave no sign they understood his mutter—you know what stones they can be—but when Papa came over to ask what they wanted I knew something was up. He stared. Papa never did that, thought it bad manners. But this time he looked at the squaw like he could go right through her and come out the other side.

They were in town to barter ponies, speaking only a little Spanish besides their own lingo. They bought some yard goods—broadcloth and denim—also a pair of wide-awakes. I remember wondering if that huge woman could ever hold a needle in her paw. They paid in silver and packed the goods in their big saddlebags.

It was after they'd ridden off that Strap and Papa took to laughing and I understood that I had just seen my first squaw-man, someone who chose the staff instead of the tomahawk, had married a brave, had plucked out the hair on the face and would, sometime or other, squat down and pretend to have a baby.

Well, I stood around in a blue terror all afternoon, doing no work, my mind roaring. How could a man turn into a woman? How could "she" marry? How come he wasn't lynched or thrown into jail? But under these confusions were greater ones. Could the laws of nature be changed, right down to the sacredest of all, the law governing the God-given character of male and female? And if that was possible, where did I fit in?

I wrestled with these matters day after day. I went to my favorite place by the river and prayed for guidance. I went up to the mound where they were erecting the new courthouse and invoked the spirit of Liberty. I did my sums and racked my brain over a new kind of amative accounting: was I a true-sexed man or was I like the squaw-man? And if the latter, could I find a place to live where God would not punish me?

In my confusion I even imagined that I was half-male and half-female, a hybrid like the Sphinx of Egypt, facing both north and south. On which side of the great divide of the sexes was I to enroll myself?

Now, looking back, I see that this was all part of my life's work, which was to see the world in a new way, not as others did, not in the accustomed mode, but with my own vision, the vision of intermediacy. This was my chore, my destiny, but in the days and weeks after I met the man-woman, it was a chore too heavy for me. So I wandered around town, rode the new municipal railway until the horses and drivers quit for the night, watched the masons fit the granite slabs onto the great building atop Travis Avenue . . . and shuddered deep in my bones. Sometimes, at midday, I felt I was standing in the hollow of a dark and starless night.

At the same time, believe it or not, the rest of my life went on without a hitch. I graduated from high school, winning the prize book. I went to fancy dress balls, Leap Year parties, Mardi Gras celebrations and even reigned once as King at the Southern Frolic of the Minerva Club. At this time I went to work full time at the store. In honor of this Papa added, very proudly, "and Son" to the sign. (The day would come when he would have to paint it out.) And I was of value to him, improving his stock of goods, elevating the grade of patronage, so that people rode in from a hundred miles around to investigate our shelves. You see how complicated my life was, how many layers of deception, hard work and confusion were built up.

I believe this was the happiest period of Mamma's life. We were all grown—you fixing to get married, Jennie—and her hardest times were over. There was running water in the house, silver and gold in her purse. The years when she couldn't sit down all day were behind her. Of course, Mamma wouldn't show her joy too plainly. She was not in the habit. Sometimes I think all might have been different had I not been raised by parents who were well-nigh wordless. Things might have been discussed, I might not have been so estranged, the doctors would not have been brought in. But that is water over the dam.

After the store closed evenings I would often take a long ramble through the less respectable part of town. It was a section of dim paths, saloons, cheap hotels and yards where Mexicans fought their roosters. I would pick some bar or alley and talk to strangers, listening to them gab about life up North, about prizefights and millionaires, about New York and Chicago and where the gold had run out in California. These distant places seemed highly exciting. To think I might step out of the house without meeting someone who had rode picket with Papa or bought a pair of britches from Belansky and Son that didn't fit right! Without running into anyone but strangers, millions of them!

Sometimes you'd ask about these nocturnal excursions, Jennie. I always made up fibs but you were kind enough not to let on. What you didn't know was how I longed to tell you where I'd been, how I felt. Longed to sit on your bed, on the pretty flowered comfort, and open my heart. But I was afraid. Afraid you'd tell Henry, who was clearly going to be a perfect mate—a go-getter and provider—but not sympathetic to such as me. So I held my tongue.

To only one person in those years did I open up, and then not very much. Do you remember Eugene Beckmann, who ran the printing and stationer's on Twelfth Street? He had come over from Germany in the early seventies—a kind, friendly man with greenish eyes and not much of a chin. Strange to say, I often encountered Mr. Beckmann on my nocturnal rounds. He seemed to prefer the company of journeymen and drummers to that of his wife and children. He always greeted me in the friendliest way and one night, when I was downcast, I expressed some of my confusion to him. He listened patiently, his green eyes fixed on my face, then replied, "Harris, we must have each the courage and independence to be ourselves." That was all—he hurried away a moment later as if he had said too much—but it remained in my memory until another time.

But it is not of the kindness of Mr. Beckmann I wish to speak now but of the events that precipitated the tragedy. Not that it looked like tragedy when it first appeared, a year or two later, in the natty, light-weight person of Jack Kilrain.

And now, after introducing Jack, I will take a breather.

It is a lovely autumn day, Sister, after much cloudiness. Often my friends here ask me what Texas was like back then when the country was young. They jaw about the frontier and the Wild West. I always reply that the States were young but not the people. I have never seen such tired souls as in Gideon—tired from work, fighting, childbearing, heat. Life was thin as skimmed milk. Do you remember the time Mamma fainted while pumping water out back, and no one to find her until Sam did? She was worn out from fifty years, and never a bit of hair coloring to keep her pretty. No, I tell my city friends, this was never a young country. Most inhabitants were bone-tired when they arrived and got tireder until they gave out for good.

Well, to return to my narrative.

By the time I met Jack Kilrain I had had a few "adventures." Once I had gone upstairs to a room at the Maverick Hotel—after more than a bit of whiskey down below—with a traveling revival preacher who wanted to give me a Bible. (It has been my experience that preachers are the most lascivious of men, which is perhaps why they took to religion in the first place.) Another time I met a clean-looking tramp named Josiah Flynt on one of my strolls through the new railyards to the south and we climbed into one of the cars that smelled of cattle. Another time I went riding with a bicycle salesman, and we ended at my hideout by the river. How these men spotted my confusion I don't know, but they did.

These escapades were mostly explorations. I knew how hellfire can scorch a sinner and I was determined to resist—but at the last moment only. Before that I wanted as much carnal pleasure as possible. Of course, my companions were always furious at my balk and tried by words, muscle or threat to seduce me. No one succeeded until I met Jack.

He appeared in the store on a day much like this one—clear and cool—while I was cutting some bombazine for a customer. By that time we had moved the yard goods to the new second storey, constructed of cottonwood planks and added on to the original log structure. Downstairs we were selling not only foodstuffs but spiritous liquors—a thriving enterprise, head and front in the business world.

He was slightly built, with small delicate hands and a beardless face. His hair was long, down to his collar, the same color as yellow-jack molasses candy. Instead of the usual rusty suit he wore a blazer. He looked like a magazine illustration. Even the golden sunburst in his lapel, the emblem of the Fenian Brotherhood, seemed more like a brooch than anything else, having lost its revolutionary fierceness. His eyes were the color of bluebonnets.

He stood watching me until I looked up. When I did, my cut went jagged and the customer let out the usual howl. "I'm looking for Mr. Belansky," he said, "I represent the Hudson Finery and Notions Company of New York City."

He spoke in a pleasant, musical voice, but I had the impression that underneath he was skittish, a touch-nervous sort of fellow. "I'm Harris Belansky," I replied, "but I reckon you want my father."

"I want anyone who can place an order for the finest lace made this side of Paris, France."

Just then Papa came up and the stranger reintroduced himself. He spoke his name clearly before handing Papa his card. I could tell, inside a few minutes, that Papa wasn't going to buy. Either he didn't like the drummer or the goods or he was in a bad mood. I waited until everything was back in the gripsack and Jack Kilrain was standing dejected in the middle of the room. By that time we were alone. "Come back tomorrow," I said, rounding the counter, "I'll talk to my father. He listens to me when it comes to ladies' apparel."

"I wasn't planning to stay another day but if you think . . ."

"I do think, Mr. Kilrain."

"Jack."

And that's how it started, the cause of my misfortune—or so I figured at the time. We shook hands on it. His was slender and thin, with almost woman's fingers. I directed him to a decent hotel for which he thanked me in his musical voice. After he left I stood woolgathering for several minutes. Something was pressing against my mind and I was trying to fight it off.

It was while Hannah and Lillie were fixing things on the table that night that I got up, just like that. I didn't want any supper, not even the floating island, my favorite dessert.

I couldn't stay put. I headed east, as usual.

I found him on the gallery of the Maverick, holding on to one of the posts. Off to one side was a group of men talking among themselves. Jack jumped the four steps to the street and gave me a smile. "Those men," he nodded back, "I believe they're criminals, they're talking about robbing a bank."

I had to laugh. "There's nobody in Gideon but black sheep and swindlers. One morning my father set down at breakfast with four murderers."

That was Papa's favorite story, true or not I couldn't say.

Well, Jack Kilrain, despite his being on the road for most of the year, was a baby about some things. "I don't know why the company sends me here," he said after we'd started to walk, "the people here have no more use for lace than for opera glasses." He looked like he was going to cry. I patted his arm.

"Don't worry. In a few years they'll all be wearing hats and shirtwaists and gowns trimmed with lace. Gideon is keeping up with the times."

He shook his head, still looking like he was going to bawl. "The worst thing is, I don't have anybody to talk to." He turned and stared at me with his bluebonnet eyes and I felt a strange linkage. I didn't have anybody to talk to either. All of a sudden I remembered the squaw-man. Was it possible that Jack Kilrain, seller of sundries, might have some knowledge he could impart to me? That he might answer some of my questions? Yet I knew I had to be careful. I turned the conversation in the direction of New York City. He was glad to talk about it. He told me about the tall buildings, the shipping, the ferries, the parades. Especially the latter. He was a great admirer of parades.

"We got election parades, militia parades, St. Patrick's parades, torchlight parades, streetcleaner parades, just about every kind you can imagine," he said as we walked up Brazos, a collection of mudholes in those days. "Yessir, Harry, you haven't seen anything till you've seen the Highlanders or the Grenadiers or the Zouaves marching up Broadway with the bands playing."

"I reckon I never will see them," I replied. "Papa would never let me go."

"That's a shame. There's lots to see in New York City if you know where to look for it. Most greenhorns don't know but I'd be happy to show you."

"Could I find employment?" The question just popped into my head.

"You'd have 'em snappin' at your heels. I might even get you a job at our factory."

He was all warmed up, his little hands going like pinwheels. "In the evening we'd go out."

"Where?"

"The Rialto. You can find whatever you want in the Rialto. Theaters, museums for men only, drinking palaces, gambling joints, poolrooms, beer gardens . . ." He laughed. "It's where the highfliers go for a good time."

By this time we'd walked to where the town petered out. Ahead was nothing but shacks and the graveyard. "I would like to see the Rialto," I said.

He edged closer. "You can find anything in the Rialto, Harry. Anything at all." The full moon had just risen to the southwest. Jack's yellow shock picked up the light.

"Like what?" My heart had started a strange hammering.

"Anything you want." He danced away, then came back. "Am I going to see your Papa again tomorrow?" It was sort of a holdup. Jack wouldn't tell me what I wanted to hear until he had his order.

"Yes," I said. And then, as sly as him, I added, "Will we take a walk tomorrow night?"

"Sure we will, Harry." His head was bathed in yellow light. "Just you and me."

He talked more about New York City after we turned around and headed back, but I was unable to reply. My heart was hammering too hard.

It went as planned. Papa listened to me and gave Jack an order not just for lace but for velvet ribbons, silk petals, bow-knots, tulle and I don't remember what else, all on my say-so. These trimmings, I believe, started Gideon on a whole new road of fashionable dress. (It might even have led to the building of the Opera House—the ladies had to have somewhere to show off.) When Jack closed his order book, with Papa's signature, he gave me a wink. That meant he'd be waiting for me. Papa's back was turned and he was muttering in his beard but I felt positive he could hear my heart.

The evening that would change the course of my life was a fine one. It was May, not too hot yet, and clear. The hills to the west had their purplish mist—the violet crown of Gideon—at sunset. As I walked toward Jack's hotel I passed no one but a speckled bitch having her pups on the street and some Mexicans with silver in their ears. Respectable people were in their homes and boardinghouses eating supper. I was alone with my fear. Pretty soon I'd be alone with Jack Kilrain. I'd already made up my mind to walk him to the edge of town again.

He was waiting on the gallery, like before, but tonight he was wearing a fine Panama. He told me Panamas were all the rage in New York City. He let me hold it, noticing the soft mesh, the lightness, but it didn't fit me. My head was a good deal larger than his—half an inch around, I guessed.

We swung up Brazos, Jack humming under his breath. Then he began to talk about the Sullivan-Ryan fight which he had seen as he was passing through Mississippi City. He'd had a good spot on the hotel porch and watched the whole bout, all eleven minutes of it. He took pride in Sullivan because of his Irish parentage, and cheered a long time when he floored his opponent. But I listened impatiently. I wanted to get back to our conversation of the night before.

"I've been thinking about New York City," I opened up. "I think I would like to see it."

He repeated his offer to show me around, with additional warnings about the dangers. He sounded a little conceited tonight—maybe getting the order from Papa had gone to his head. I steered the talk to the Rialto again, saying it sounded pretty lively. He laughed at that,

kind of sharp. "You'll find everything there except a church, Harry."
He looked at me. "You'll even find a circus."

"Oh we have circuses right here in Gideon," I rejoined, thinking
about the Grand Continental which was due for its annual visit in a
few weeks.

That elicited another laugh. "That ain't the kind I'm talking about."

"What kind is that, Jack?"

He wiped his mouth delicately with his skinny finger. "I'm talking
about males and females in the sexual act."

"You can see that?"

"If you know where to look. And can pay for it."

I believe that even now, more than half a century later, some corner
of me is shocked by that. Maybe I am still a young man, trembling
with fear and ignorance, walking with Jack Kilrain past the land-
locator's office out to where the town gave way to Mexican shacks and
tombstones. Because as I sit here by the window on 44th Street I can
still feel the whirling in my head, feel the ground shaking, feel Jack's
shadowy eyes on me.

In the next instant something passed between us. I cannot name it
but I have experienced it many times since with other strangers. It is a
form of wordless communication, of perfect understanding.

He stepped toward me and laid his hand on my arm. "You know,
Harry, on the Rialto you can find young fellows dressed up as girls.
That's right, togged up in feminine apparel."

I almost stopped breathing, remembering the squaw-man.

"They call 'em French doll-babies and they have girl's names like
Jennie, Eunice, Phyllis, June. There are places where they go regular."

Jack's face was right close to me. I could smell the Pear's soap on
his skin.

"I think you'd like to see those doll-babies, Harry."

"No I wouldn't." I twisted away but he held on.

"Yes you would. I knew it the minute I laid eyes on you."

This time I didn't pull away. Something in me was softening up. "I
. . . I don't want to hear any more about it."

"Yes you do. You want to hear all about it. Just like you were there
and could see it for yourself."

It is very hard for me to write about what happened next, yet I want
to. Much of it, however, is just a blurred set of movements in my
mind.

The fact is, before I could stop myself, before I even knew it was happening, I was kissing Jack Kilrain on the lips. Smack on the mouth. I don't believe either of us made the first move. We just kind of come together with a light and force that must have been moving underground all our lives. And pretty soon we were so worked up there was no stopping us.

Jack wasn't like the corrupt preacher nor the little tramp nor anybody else. Our loving seemed natural and, well, pure. Pure because we were doing it under the moon and stars, below the crown of Temple Mount. Because both of us were lonesome. Because we were young. And so I didn't pull back, not once. When it was over—and it was over mighty quick—I felt grand.

We sat back, in the swept yard behind a deserted shack, looking at each other. Jack was crying a little. He didn't seem at all proud of himself now. "Two hearts in parley, Harry," is what he said.

I didn't reply, just sat there wondering what would happen now.

After resting awhile, we began to talk in earnest. I told Jack about the circus and Enzo and Dr. Santvoord, also about Papa and Mamma and all of you. It seemed that for the first time in my life I could begin to understand myself. In turn, he told me about his own family—a brood of eight, fatherless, all struggling to survive. I also told him about the squaw-man and he described the nancies of the Rialto, the evenings he had spent among them, the sign of the red necktie that some of them wear.

When we tired of talking, we touched each other again, only this time it was better because we knew each other. I never thought skin could be so smooth nor parts so delicious. I was filled with emotion. It seemed I had crossed the threshold to which all my years of delirious imaginings had been the prelude. Even when Jack proposed that I perform an act I had not previously considered possible, I did not hesitate. I united my flesh, my instincts, with his. I have no words to describe the extraordinary charm of his warm, smooth flank. It seemed that all we did was done for the first time in the history of the world.

It was a while after that, when the moon was getting low, that he urged me to come north. He spoke of many interesting things—of trysting places where people such as he and I were accustomed to foregather, where there were marble-topped tables, orchestras and a floor free for dancing. He spoke of the ease with which you might catch the eye of like-minded fellows — before a shop window or at a bench in Madison Park — and begin a conversation that would move on to confidentialities. He told me about the personals column in the newspapers by means of which you might invite correspondence. I could hardly believe my ears. There seemed to be another world waiting for me, one in which I truly belonged.

At the same time, warnings sounded. How could I live among strangers and Yankees? Weren't there thieves, blackmailers, murderers in every corner of the metropolis? But more than that, my emotions were at war within me. Jack had painted a picture, so I thought, of unrestrained lust, of surrender to morbid passions. What would happen to me if I gave in? In my ignorance I thought I knew the answer to that: nervous degeneration, hyperesthesia, insanity. Lying there in the chill May night, Jack Kilrain's face indistinct beside me, I was once again a picture of confusion. One part of me wanted to leave Gideon, say goodbye to family, head north. Another part wanted to stay put, resist the urges draggingat me, make Papa proud.

And underneath these thoughts, which bucked and pitched in my head, was another question: *Where on this earth did I fit in?*

We walked back to the hotel not saying much. Jack was weary, I was frozen stiff. It had been a long night; our vital energies had been drained off. Soon the boardinghouses would be ringing their bells for breakfast. After that Jack would ride the Great Northern out of town. Everything would be as before.

But I was wrong to believe that, because I had overlooked one mischance: Mr. Buckner of the livery stable. A man of no set hours, delivering and retrieving his conveyances day or night. And now, at cockcrow, Mr. Buckner was riding his big old claybank up the street. He saw us and stopped, spoke politely. Papa was one of his best customers, after all. But there was something in his stare, the set of his jaw. Maybe he saw the dirt-sweepings on our elbows and britches. Maybe he saw guilt in our eyes. Maybe he saw something else he couldn't name. But by the time he posted off I had a feeling there'd be trouble. "I think you better go while you can," I said to Jack. "I'm going home."

He called after me, laughing and reassuring, but I didn't turn around. My legs had turned to straw and my head was pounding. Something terrible was going to happen. I knew Gideon and he didn't.

By the time I got home my night with Jack, the promises we had made, had been swallowed up. I even believe that when I reached the house—at the very moment Mr. Buckner was walking out the front door with Papa behind him in his nightshirt—I thought I deserved punishment. But if so, the desire was buried deep within me. A lie was quick to my lips.

"Where have you been, Harris?" Papa was looking exceptionally old this morning, perhaps because of what August Buckner had told him.

"I spent the night with Jennie and Henry."

"Jennie and Henry?"

"Yessir."

He gazed at me in the hardest way, as if he could tunnel through to the truth, but I was experienced at looking innocent. He put the question again and I repeated my answer with a steady voice.

"You have not been . . ." he sought the word but could not find it. Papa could never find it when he needed it.

"No sir. I have been sleeping all the night on their new sofa in the parlor." I planned to get over to your place double-quick, Jennie, as soon as Papa released me.

We stood silent for a moment, Papa chewing his beard, and then said, "August has gone over to the hotel where your friend is staying."

"Right this minute?"

I believe my answer betrayed me because Papa's eyes grew huge. The next instant I was as nonchalant as before. "I don't believe Mr. Buckner will find him because he planned to leave first thing."

"When did he tell you that?"

"Last night. I saw him for a few minutes after supper."

"After supper?"

"Yes."

It was a barefaced lie and not a good one. If I had had more time I would have invented a better. Unless this time I wanted to be caught out.

At any rate, it didn't matter. Jack had not left. Mr. Buckner found him at the breakfast table eating slapjacks. They had a talk. In return for letting him go scot-free, Jack informed on everything that had passed between us. After that Mr. Buckner escorted him to the depot. I found this out later—several days later. Because until then nobody spoke to me. I remained in limbo. Mamma, you might remember, couldn't stop weeping, and made no attempt to break through the wall of silence. During these days I had plenty of time to think.

My thoughts went first to Jack Kilrain. After my first anger passed, I knew I could not blame him for blabbing. He had no doubt been threatened with everything from a whipping to the federal marshal. His livelihood, and that of his family, depended on his keeping on the good side of the merchants. You know how fast news travels. And he was a lightweight person to begin with—I had spotted that right off. I forgave him at last. Not without, at first, much bitterness.

My thoughts then went to the stories Jack had told me. I tried to picture the Rialto as he described it—a stretch of street that glittered in my fancy like the heavenly city. As I imagined it, it grew in reality and nearness. It actually seemed to float toward me as I did chores around the house, getting bigger and bigger until it had replaced Gideon altogether. I also tried to picture the inverts—it was a word Jack had used more than once—with their red neckties, white gloves and patent-leather shoes. What were they like? How did they earn their keep? Were they considered monsters of wickedness? These were questions to which I would have the answers sooner than I thought.

At last, after almost a week of captivity, Papa announced to me in private that he had arranged an interview with a Dr. Graham. This doctor was superintendent at the state hospital, though this was not told me at the time. I was only informed that we would visit those premises to discuss my malady. There were many cures available; it was only a matter of finding the right one.

Naturally my reaction was one of fear. My previous experience with medical men had not been good. And this man was an alienist, specializing in diseases of the mind. What was the fate that awaited me?

We drove the six miles north to the asylum, which had been newly enlarged for the accommodation of more patients. At this time there were over two hundred. Although I had seen the building many times, on this trip it looked different—vaster and more sinister, its Greek portico and high dome seeming more like a tomb than a place for curing human souls. I asked Papa several times in the course of the journey what was to happen, stating clearly that I would not consent to be immured behind those walls. He assured me that we were only going to consult the great Dr. Graham. He then went on, in his kindliest voice, to say that if I did not mend my ways, I would miss the greatest happiness available to a young man—marriage and the rearing of children. He said this in a voice that broke several times. He was much stirred, as was I, and I gave him my word that I would cooperate with whatever course of treatment was decided for me. I meant it. I did want to overcome my defect. It had caused me no end of suffering and I foresaw that worse was to come. How right I was.

After tying up we stood for a moment looking up at the great grim building. Papa's face was deeply lined; I believe the events of the past week had aged him by several years. What they had done to me I have already said.

Dr. Graham was in one of the wards when we arrived and we were asked to wait in his office. Behind the main building, in an enclosed area, we could see patients strolling about. Several attendants were visible. It was an airing court where they were permitted to take sunshine, we were told. Several, I noticed, were wearing strait-waistcoats. I pointed this out to Papa who chose not to look.

Dr. Graham was a pleasant-looking man of middle height and ample figure. He spoke courteously to both of us. I saw no reason to mistrust him. He seemed very different from the madman who had prescribed the canvas corset years ago—prefacing that, you will recall, with a sermon on eternal damnation. Dr. Graham, by contrast, was a man of moderation. This was clear as he spoke of the improvements he had instituted in the regimen of the asylum—amateur theatricals, calisthenic dances, magic-lantern shows, readings, socials, "There are some," he concluded, "who believe that the insane cannot be cured. Who therefore don't bother to follow the routines that would promote recovery. Here we treat our patients with skill, humanity and devotion. We have had some remarkable successes."

I wondered why he should give us this advertisement for his wares. We had not come to sample them. He went on to speak of the causes of mental alienation. "I am convinced," he observed, "that excesses of all kinds contribute to this disease. Excess of alcohol or tobacco or nervous stimulants. Or," and he turned his gaze fully on me, "other things which may cause nervous exhaustion and disturb the equilibrium of life. Anything that uses up vital power, if persisted in, can lead to mental aberration."

I shifted nervously and looked at Papa. He was sweating slightly. I decided I had nothing to lose by speaking up.

"Among your modern courses of treatment," I said, surprised at the vigor of my tone, "what do you recommend for people in my case?"

"Well, Harris, that depends." His reply was slow and smooth. "It depends on whether they are cooperative or not." I waited and he continued. "In cases of willful perversion, which is much like inebriation or opium-eating, we take strong measures." He glanced at Papa, who nodded slightly. "There is surgical treatment to eliminate the instinct itself. There are operations, less severe, that reverse sexual feeling." He smiled reassuringly. "But in cases where there is neither stubbornness nor hereditary taint, we take milder corrective measures."

"What are those?"

He sat back. His chair creaked. Papa was staring fixedly at a spot on the wall. "We might begin with a regimen of cold sitz baths followed by a course of intellectual training. This would require seclusion from the world, at least for a time. Removal from familiar surroundings, with change of habit and associations, can often modify the disease."

I looked around. I certainly did not want to be secluded in this place. But there was nothing to worry about — Papa had given me his word.

"Another possibility," Dr. Graham continued, affable as before, "is Mesmerism. We have had some very good results, although the course of treatment may be quite lengthy. In one case resembling yours, Harris, Dr. Schrenk required one hundred and fifty sittings." He paused and regarded me amiably. "There were other requirements too, which I will not mention just now."

"Well, I would have no objection to that," I replied, "provided we could do it somewhere in town. This is rather a long drive."

He nodded pleasantly. "There are also milder treatments. One of my colleagues has great faith in the power of bicycle riding."

"Bicycle riding?" It was almost the first time Papa had spoken.

"Yes, Mr. Belansky. Bicycles are excellent in the treatment of nervous diseases, especially abnormally developed sexual appetite. We had a case here last year where a young man the same age as your son was able to control himself by taking a hard ride several times a day."

I started to laugh, then checked myself. I was not in humorous surroundings. "Well, I'm game for that too. When do we get started?"

"There's no time like the present," said Dr. Graham, with his amiable smile. He stood up. Papa and I did the same. My mind was busy. Hypnotism and bicycle-riding—the wonders of modern science! Could such methods really banish the images that were constantly exhibiting themselves to me? Was my indifference to the opposite sex about to end? I grasped at these ideas even while common sense told me to disregard them.

"Harris, would you remain here while I speak to your father privately?"

Smelling no treachery, I nodded. While waiting, my gaze moved to a grimy poster in one corner—a depiction of the brain, a chart of bumps. I wondered if my own cranial bulges would reveal to an expert what I already knew to be true—that my mental faculties veered toward the voluptuous, the mirthful, the secretive and the self-esteeming. Well, it didn't matter. My character traits would not end by naming them.

The next moment the door behind me flung open. Two powerful attendants rushed in and seized me, one on each side. I was lifted from my chair as if I had been a matchstick. One of them snarled, "You going to come easy or do we jacket you?"

The words made no sense and I didn't reply. They heaved at me until I was passed through a small door I had not noticed. We were in a long passage. The air was hot, fetid. Soon this opened into another building.

By this time I had found my voice. One of my captors told me to quit my yelling but I didn't. My mind was going off like a firecracker. Suddenly a barred door appeared. It was opened and I was pushed into a cell about six by ten feet. There was nothing in it but a bed with a husk mattress. The door clanged shut behind me, a key turned and I stood, heart exploding, in a state bordering on mania.

This had all happened so fast I had lost my bearings. Now I realized I was in an area surrounded by cages like my own, whose occupants were hallooing, banging and screeching at me. I stepped up to the bars of my own and roared louder than anyone. I had been decoyed and betrayed—and my own father had arranged it all! I can hardly describe my emotions at that moment. I cursed all of you. I cursed life itself. When my throat was hoarse I retreated to the bed and howled. It was the end of my life. I was then twenty-one years old.

And now begins the strangest episode in this strange journey of mine. But I will end these retrospections for the time being. They have become too burdensome to be recalled.

Two days have gone by since writing here. In that time I have been visited by several friends, like me put out to pasture, and by the young doctor. There is, I believe, nothing new to be said of my health, so I will pick up the thread of my story, trying not to suffer too much in the retelling.

I was left entirely alone that first day except for an attendant who fed me some thin soup and bread—standing and watching while I ate, and removing the plate afterward. It was almost impossible to sleep, even after I calmed down, due to the unearthly sounds all around, as well as to the highly vitiated air, saturated with medicinal odors and body effluvia—the most disgusting combination imaginable.

The following morning, after a deplorable breakfast, I looked up to find Dr. Graham standing outside my cage. He observed me in an amiable way, as if this were the most natural place in the world for me. "Did you sleep well, Harris?" he asked.

Something went haywire in me and I leaped and wailed at him as if I were as mad as the people around me. Perhaps, at that moment, I was. He stood calmly, his smile fixed. When I finished he said, "You know, Harris, we are here to help you, but you must cooperate. Patients who are not obedient to our requests are usually sorry later."

That set me off again. I accused him of every treachery. This time he didn't listen long. With a nod at some attendants, he walked off. A few minutes later I was taken from my cell and dragged to the bathroom. There my clothes were stripped off and I was plunged bodily into a zinc tub full of icy water. This so convulsed me that I screamed louder, whereupon they drowned my voice by holding me under water until I was nearly dead. "Will you be obedient now?" one of them—a huge Irishman with a potato face—asked. I gave my promise, but to make my subduing complete they plunged me several more times. Then I was led, wet and shivering, to my room, past the jeers of the patients who reveled in my punishment. In my room I was given no cover, nothing to hide my nakedness. You can imagine my state of mind. I was more dead than alive. This strangulation by water constituted my baptism into hospital life.

That afternoon I was permitted to dress in hospital clothes and enter the lounge. This was a large room full of inmates lying listlessly or crouching on the floor. They wore clothing of the commonest material, often unclean, and observed me with reactions that ranged from disinterest to anger. I immediately went to one of the attendants and requested pen and paper. My intention was to write Papa, telling him how I had been treated. I was sure he had no idea of the abuse that went on. I was still innocent, you see, despite everything still turning to Papa for help.

The attendant laughed in my face. Then he told me patients were not permitted writing materials without the permission of the superintendent. When I demanded to speak to Dr. Graham, he signaled to another attendant, who stepped forward with a flask of liquid. When they poured it into a glass I smelled a heavy aroma. Of course I refused to drink, at which they jumped on me and forced it down my throat. This was my first, but not my last, dose of chloral hydrate—the commonest sedative and one which leaves you groggy for a day. By the time I was locked in my cell again, I was in a half stupor. They had no more trouble with me that day.

This routine went on for a week before I was given my first interview with the physician who would treat me. During this week, the slightest infraction resulted in either an icy plunge or a forced feeding of chloral hydrate. If these disciplines did not bring about submission, mechanical restraints were used—either the milder form, which involved locking the wrists into iron rings attached to a leather belt, or the stricter form of the strait-waistcoat. Luckily, I escaped these.

During the week I made the acquaintance of some fellow prisoners. One shriveled old man, in the cell next to mine, drank his urine each morning, saying this place smelled strongly of chloroform and this was how to counteract it. He was very deluded and melancholy. He died not long after my arrival.

Another inmate had a sad story to tell. He was a fat, red-faced young man named Koppin. He had fired four shots at a friend to whom he was passionately attached—shots intended to kill his friend and then himself commit suicide. However, he was grabbed before he could shoot himself. His friend likewise recovered. Koppin had been committed for criminal insanity, although his behavior seemed to me quite sane except for a tendency to hysterical self-reproach. Soon after his committal, his testicles had been removed. This did not seem to improve him in any way. "I am still utterly incorrigible, utterly incurable and utterly impossible," he told me one afternoon.

This seemed to be true. Each time Dr. Graham or one of the other doctors entered our ward, poor Koppin would rush up to him and start screaming at the top of his lungs, "Where are my testicles, what have you done with my testicles?" This happened several times every day—a terrible strain all around. Yet I believe he was actually a normal fellow driven mad with their cures.

As you can see, I was in an antechamber of hell, without legal recourse. I ascertained that all the forms of law had been fulfilled in committing me (on the verdict of four men, two of them physicians). Each morning on arising, when I saw the grated windows and barred doors, inhaled the fetid smells, heard the wild hallooing, I was beside myself with grief. Several times my despair was so great I tore my forearm with my fingernails. There seemed no greater injustice in the world than the one that had befallen me.

And yet I survived—survived with luck, cleverness, lying, even in a place where reason itself had been dethroned.

At last the day arrived for my first interview with Dr. Commonsworth. Prior to this I had been removed to another ward where the residents were less ferocious. It was, in fact, relatively calm, and without the prisonlike lattice on the windows. We had a good view of the hospital grounds, since we were on the first floor.

Dr. Commonsworth was a sallow man of middle years with a beard which he parted in the middle. "Welcome, Harris," he said when I turned up, with the ever-present attendant, "I hear you have been making grand progress already."

I knew this was to warm me up, make me amenable to his suggestions, but I agreed. I had already learned about agreeing with the authorities. "Yes sir, I feel better already, thanks to the treatment I have received."

He heard no sarcasm in my voice and beamed at me. Then he motioned me to a comfortable chair and dismissed the guard. As soon as I was seated I asked when I would be released.

"That depends," he replied. "We have you in our charge in order to rid your mind of certain gross impurities. As soon as that is done, we'll be glad to see the last of you."

I nodded. "I'm eager to cooperate, doctor. Can we begin at once?"

He beamed even more broadly and came around to my chair. He passed his hand several times across my forehead while speaking in a low voice. I closed my eyes. If he was going to practice hypno-science,

I would make it as easy as possible for him. "I do not want you to think of me as a doctor," he murmured in a soothing voice I was to become familiar with, "but as your friend, Harris, whom you can trust as you trust yourself."

He continued in that vein for a while, then asked me to lie on the settee in the corner. He went to the windows and closed the curtains. The room became dim; I felt a pleasant weariness in my limbs. He returned and took a seat behind my head, continuing to speak about friendship and trust. Gradually he moved on to the subject of love. "Love is the most precious emotion that you can feel, Harris," he murmured, "love for your fellow creatures, for your parents, for the Almighty." He paused, sighed, then went on to describe the love that a man feels for a woman. "This love," he said, "is the most sacred opportunity of all because it is part of God's plan for the human race."

He touched my forehead and then urged me to go to sleep. This was urged over and over in the same mild voice. But even as my lethargy deepened, as my limbs became numb, I knew I would not pass into the state of trance required. Something in me would not permit it. Thus my faculties remained alert, even as I gave the drowsy responses he wanted. Yes, a happy marriage was now the goal of my life. My abnormal attachments were ending. I repented of my former behavior. I would acquire a natural desire for the opposite sex.

After each session, Dr. Commonsworth would wake me up with a clap of his hands. "How do you feel now, Harris?" he would ask. I would stagger up as if I had been truly asleep and reply that I felt "less morbid." He would beam and clap me on the shoulder. "It's the exaltation of your willpower," he would cry, "we'll have you out of here in no time!"

One day toward the end of our third week, he told me that the responsibility he felt toward me during my "sleep" was greater than that felt by father or mother, teacher or preacher, husband or wife. We were, he said, fashioning a new creature. It was a form of birth. I would then thank him profusely for his kindness, to which he would reply, "Don't thank me, Harris, I am merely the viceregent of the Almighty."

After I returned to my ward, I would reflect on my future. It became clear to me that these sleep-sessions might continue for years. Dr. Graham, in our first interview, had mentioned the figure 150. And was there any guarantee that I would be considered cleansed, my old instincts eradicated, even then? Might it not take a lifetime?

Dr. Commonsworth, at some of our sessions, had dropped hints about more drastic measures. From talking to other inmates I learned of extreme courses ranging from an operation on the filaments of the pudic nerve to vasectomy to the annihilation applied to poor Koppin. Each of these ideas terrified me.

By this time I had been able to write several times to Papa. I had received replies, invariably counseling patience and perseverance, as well as giving news of the family and the store. He had visited twice, also full of good counsel, and paying no attention to my tales of horror. I now believe that, in his stoic way, he believed that pain was an indication of progress. He left each time (after a short talk with Dr. Graham) convinced he was doing the right thing.

I remember the exact moment when my desire to leave the asylum hardened into a fierce resolve to effect it myself. It happened while I was on Dr. Commonsworth's couch, listening to him extol the virtues of the female form. It was one of those moments in life when suddenly you *know*. I would be numbered among the insane forever— never again considered a fit associate for family and friends—unless I took matters in my own hands. I ceased listening, ceased responding, as the conviction spread through me like a lake of fire: *it was up to me.*

Dr. Commonsworth, realizing I was not in the usual "trance," asked me the reason for my resistance. I mumbled that I missed talking to sane people. "Never fear, Harris," he replied soothingly, "that day will come sooner than you think."

"Yes," I vowed to myself, even while repeating his last phrase aloud to mollify him, "it will, it will." In the next instant, my plan was complete.

By this time I had been in the hospital for three months and it was apparent to the attendants and staff that I was not a maniac. I had made myself useful in many ways—helping with unruly patients, offering to empty night-pots, refill wet mattress ticks, wash and comb the more helpless, etc. For these favors I was often allowed to roam the grounds alone. In fact, I was sometimes asked to keep an eye on the other inmates while the guards went to the kitchen for coffee— an assignment strictly against the rules. Of course, all of us were kept within bounds by a high concrete wall.

On this particular day (it was August 9, a day I will never forget, hot as blazes) I was asked to take some of my ward-mates outside. Because of the heat, there being no sunshade out there, they didn't want to go. This made my plan even easier of execution. I had chosen the exact place for my shinny over the fence—behind the laundry, where a twenty-foot standpipe carried water from the tank into the interior. I had been fortunate enough, a few days before, to secure a straw hat and a jacket of twilled cotton—cast aside by one of the dayworkers who toiled in the kitchen. These would disguise my hospital costume once I reached the outside world. I fixed my hour of escape at three-thirty, when the heat would be most intense.

It wanted now only a least bit of patience. As I sat on my bed for the last time (I hoped), looking about the high chamber which had housed thirty of us for these past months, I felt a sudden sadness. Some of my companions in the Sixth Ward were among the best company and most original thinkers I had ever met. They had taught me much about human existence. Some of them, including a man who called himself Jesus, and another who had foretold the War Between the States thirty years ago, had become my friends. I would never see them again. I would never know of their progress or decay. Our paths had crossed and now would part.

But just as suddenly as it came, my sadness lifted. A new power of resolve (quite different from my childish willfulness) surged through me. I could feel the old Harris sloughing away in the face of the trials ahead. It may seem difficult of belief, but at that moment I was almost happy. I had broken the chains of family and society—chains which had come as close to strangulating me as had the plunges in the zinc tubs. My allegiance to Papa, to Mamma, to house and store, to Gideon and even to the state of Texas, were about to end. I had only one purpose in life: to find freedom.

Not that I harbored many illusions about the future. I saw quite clearly, while sitting on my cot, that the years ahead would be mean and poor. They might end in catastrophe. Certainly they would take me into exile. But in acknowledging that I could count on no one but myself I had made a great stride forward. Looking back on that reverie, I believe it constituted the precise moment when I accepted the fact that I fit in nowhere in the world except the place that I would make for myself. Why that should have made me happy is hard to understand, but it did.

Of my escape little need be said. I slipped out in midafternoon, when all were resting, and had no trouble getting up the standpipe.

The concrete wall had been set with spikes but these didn't stop me. Within five minutes of leaving I was on the road to town, my straw hat pulled low, my jacket covering up my dirty grey shirt. I would have looked suspicious to anyone driving by, but in the heat no one did. By early evening (after a rest in a chinaberry grove) I was at the outskirts of town. I attracted little attention. I was helped in this by the fact that Papa had given out the story that I was gone to St. Louis for training in modern business methods. Those who recognized me did not dream I was an escaped patient.

I knew exactly what to do, where to go, having thought about it long and hard over the past few days.

I knocked at the side door of Eugene Beckmann's shop about five. One of his apprentices opened it — a boy I did not know. He didn't like my looks and went to close it, but I forced my way in. He was dealing with the new Harris Belansky, you see. Five minutes later I was in Mr. Beckmann's private office, pouring out my story. He never took his green eyes from my face as he listened. When I told of the forced sedatives, the icy baths, the dark room, the strong box and all the other things I had encountered, he closed his eyes and rubbed them, as if he did not want to see. I could hardly blame him.

"If I had known, Harris, if I had known . . ." he shook his head. I knew what he wanted to say, that he would have rescued me, but we both knew that was impossible. Then he clenched his fists and started to revile Papa, calling him unnatural and unfeeling. "I wish I had been your father," he said, "I would have taught you. . ."

But I interrupted him. None of that mattered now. What I wanted was his help. "I will need two hundred dollars in silver, Mr. Beckmann. I will pay you back when I can."

He said he didn't have that much cash in the safe but that he would make a withdrawal from the bank next day. He would do it before regular business hours, however, so that I would not be unduly delayed.

"Then I will sleep here," I said, looking around the cluttered premises. "If you will let me."

He nodded eagerly. "I will make up a pallet for you."

After some more avowals of support and friendship, Mr. Beckmann dismissed the other workers and helped me get settled. Several times he looked at me in a troubled way, as if he had something on his mind. I had a suspicion what it was but I made no effort to help him. At the same time, I wondered if I could trust him. I had, after all, suffered much from the treachery of my elders. Still, I had no choice. He was my only hope.

At last he said good night and left, locking me in. I would go supperless to bed, I thought. But that did not turn out to be the case. By moonrise, Mr. Beckmann was back, with some selections from his own family table—collard greens, ham and sweet-potato pie, still warm. I ate in the dark, to avoid the possibility of any night-callers dropping in, while he sat near by. Now it is coming, I thought, what he wanted to tell me. Now I will hear his story, as he heard mine.

And I did. Eugene Beckmann told me many interesting things that night, as the moon flooded through the window and onto our ghostly faces, but I will not repeat any of them here. This is, after all, my story—I have no right to tell that of anyone else. But let me say that after he finished I understood why he had spent so many evenings rambling through the east end of town, talking to strangers, and why he was so moved by my own plight.

Eugene Beckmann was my greatest friend and benefactor—the first outside the family. Had it not been for his goodness, I might have stayed in the asylum forever, losing whatever of mind I had. I was truly saddened to learn of his death by meningitis while still quite young. His jaw became abscessed and he could not breathe—a sad end for a man who never spoke anything but kindness to me.

I took the early morning stage out of town, deciding to connect with the railroad in Mason rather than in Gideon. The one-way fare was a dollar—using the first of the Liberty Heads that Mr. Beckmann supplied, along with suit, shirt and tie. I thought I had never spent money more wisely. I stayed out of sight as we rattled out of town, but on the road I sat up and looked around. The air tasted sweet and cool. The low scrub was green. I wondered when I would see all this again. I wondered about Papa. But as the driver applied the whip and we speeded up, my thoughts let go of Gideon. I was on a new journey, a new life. Nobody could stop me now.

And now my story is done. There were many difficulties ahead, but eventually I found a place where I could earn a living, thanks in no small part to my experience in Papa's store. (Jack Kilrain, by the way, when I looked him up, did not aid me much, despite the promises he had made.)

Not much remains to be said. As you know, I did not make it up with Papa for almost twenty years, returning only when Mamma was in her last illness and he was languishing. He never apologized nor admitted, during these visits, that he had been in the wrong. He would not have been Papa if he could have done that. Of the old matters, the cause of our trouble, we never spoke. The book remained closed. But there was one day, of those last, that stands out in my memory.

During his last winter we took him to Austin for the annual reunion of the Texas Brigade. General Hood was long since departed (the year was 1910) but a few veterans were left. They posed for their picture on the steps of the Capitol, Papa in the second row. After the photo was snapped he called me over and presented me to his comrades one by one.

As he did so, I could see that he was truly proud. He spoke of my success in New York City. He told of his plans to visit me, to see the Statue of Liberty and Brooklyn Bridge. He said that I had taken the family name to a bigger, wider world.

He didn't come to New York, of course. But I like to picture what a visit from him would have been like. I would have shown him the marvels, then I would have sat him down in a restaurant and told him that I bore no grudge. I would have added that my life had been full of friends and good times, even though solitary in one important respect. Then I would have told him that I would not have cared to live anyone's life but my own. I think he would have understood instantly that this is the best any man can say about himself. Not that he would have replied, or smiled, or done anything but grunt into his beard. But that is the way he was. And so, I am content. Good night and God bless you. You are all in my prayers forever.

Uncle Harris' signature was large and florid—the writing of a man who signed business documents all his life. I sat for a long time, the manuscript on my knee, vaguely aware that I was expected back in the living room for a last word with Cousin Minna. But I found it difficult to move. The past lay heavily on me.

I picked up the envelope again, noting the thick red seal which I had broken. Questions tugged at me, questions which I did not bother to verbalize. If there were little mysteries connected to Uncle Harris' letter, they didn't matter. The main one had been solved. I pulled myself out of the armchair at last, letter and envelope in hand. She must have heard me coming, because she was leaning forward in her chair, gazing toward me. The dark glasses were still in place. I sat down. There was so much to say I couldn't begin.

At last I thanked her. Then, seeking to head off the larger queries in my mind, I lifted the envelope. "This envelope. It had a seal. It looked very old. I wonder if . . ."

"The seal that you broke."

"Yes."

An insect buzzed against a window. "You want to know who put the seal there."

"Yes."

"Uncle Harris did."

My thoughts skittered around. "If he put it there, then . . . then . . ." I was too surprised to continue.

"That is correct. You are the first to read the letter."

"I'm the first?" My throat constricted. "What about Jennie? He wrote it to his sister."

"There was something I didn't tell you. A note of instruction. It was clipped to the envelope."

"From Uncle Harris?"

"Yes."

I closed my eyes. "Go on, please."

"In this note he mentioned your name. He said he had made a promise to you and he wanted to keep it."

I squeezed my eyes tighter. I remembered the promise.

"And that if you ever came back here, back to Gideon to find out about him, you were to be given the letter.

I leaned my head against the back of my chair. A conversation on a lawn, forty years earlier, floated in front of me. A moment later I opened my eyes. "But if that's so, why did he address it to Jennie?"

"He wanted to tell both of you. The past and the future. It's perfectly natural. But she died soon after he did—before she could read it."

"But suppose I hadn't come back?"

"If you hadn't come back?" Cousin Minna seemed to consider this question absurd. "But you did."

"This trip was a fluke."

"Well then," she shrugged, "it would have ended up with the other papers in the Gideon Library."

I shook my head. "It's all so weird."

She removed her glasses, quite slowly, so that her black eyes shone on me. "Uncle Harris must have known something about you," she said.

"But I was only ten when he died—what could he have known?"

She didn't hear. Her mouth opened, her jaw sagged. Then she seemed to quiver all over. In the next instant Alicia rushed in.

Twenty minutes later I tiptoed out of the house. I called that evening; Cousin Minna had been taken to the hospital and was in stable condition. I left for San Francisco early the following day, after ordering flowers for her.

I keep Uncle Harris' letter to me in a safe place and reread it from time to time, especially when I am sad or angry or life seems unbearably difficult. It has marvelous restorative powers; it invariably infuses me with courage. Cousin Minna died last year at the age of 85. Unfortunately, I was not able to attend her funeral, although she was much in my thoughts, as were her city and the people in it, many of whom turned out to pay their last respects. None of them, I am quite sure, remembered Uncle Harris.

The Purple Prince

Martin saw the boy several times that fall before he spoke to him. Once the boy was wandering in a meadow with his head down. Another time the boy was riding his bike, followed by a huge Great Dane. The third time their paths crossed was Halloween, which was when they spoke.

Martin's doorbell rang. He found the boy standing on the stoop dressed as a bum. His cheeks were smudged, his front teeth blacked out and an old fedora sat on his head. Martin called to Evan, who came to the door and stood beside him.

"What are you supposed to be?" Martin asked the boy.

"I'm a tramp."

"You all by yourself?"

"I'm with Joe. He's scared."

The boy pointed to the shrubbery. A younger boy, dressed as a pirate, was standing there. He seemed to be shivering with shyness.

"Here's a quarter," said Martin, "be sure you know the people who give you candy."

"Yeah, some of them are poison." The boy looked up at the two men. One of the men thought the boy was cute and the other thought that his life would be full of hard and unpleasant things.

"I have to go now," said the boy. "There are guys with cinders in stockings running around to beat you up." He hadn't seen any such boys. They were the relic of his father's experience of Halloween in Chicago thirty-five years before.

"Well goodbye," said Martin, "say goodbye to Joe too."

But when the boy hesitated, still standing under the yellow porch light, his large eyes glistening in the smudged face, Martin said, "What's your name?"

"Donny."

The boy was glad the man had asked his name. It made everything easier. Besides, he was curious about the two men who lived where the Haddens used to live. He'd heard his parents talking about them.

"Well, be careful, Donny."

He noticed that the two men didn't close their door until he'd walked over to Joe, who was always acting stupid. Donny looked back once. The first man was waving. Donny waved back, feeling good. He wondered if the man would be a friend. This seemed unlikely; his experience with older men, based on his father and his gym teacher, was not good.

The next time Martin saw Donny was at the local library. This was a white brick building at the foot of Main Street. When he got there on a Saturday afternoon, Story Hour had just ended. Several children had been listening to a teenaged girl read *Singing Raven and the Hopi Treasure*. Martin knew this because it was shown on a sign, together with a Polaroid of the teenager, who wore pigtails and a beaded band around her forehead. He himself had used this library years ago, as a child, though he had generally avoided Indian stories. He preferred knights and squires.

Donny was the last to come down the stairs from the Children's Section. Martin, who was thumbing through the card catalog, happened to look up. At first he didn't recognize the boy without the smudges on his face and the battered fedora, but then he did. The boy had certainly recognized him, because he was leaning his chin on the banister post staring with his large eyes.

"Hello, Donny," Martin called.

"Sshh!" hissed the fat librarian.

Martin went over and put out his hand. The boy's was soft and limp. He hadn't been taught how to shake hands like a man.

"How was Story Hour?" Martin whispered.

"It was okay."

The boy spoke in a loud, breathy voice. Martin realized he didn't really know how to whisper.

Donny was very glad to see the man. He was nice-looking, with a mustache. He didn't have the starey look some grownups did. He wore soft blue clothes—blue shirt and blue pants like a cowboy. He was much nicer-looking than his father, who wore wire glasses and was kind of fat. He'd thought of the man several times since Halloween, each time picturing the man showing up in the schoolyard or in the meadow where he went to pick wildflowers. Most of all, he pictured meeting the man alone. They wouldn't get to be friends unless they could talk without a lot of people around.

"Do you come to Story Hour every week?"

That was a stupid question. He didn't know if he came every week. Sometimes he did and sometimes he didn't, that's all. He shrugged. The man blinked. Then he said, "What's that book you've got?"

Donny held out the book so the man could read the title. It was called *The Purple Prince of Oz*. He'd read it three times already and had just decided to read it again.

When Martin saw the title of book he was surprised. He didn't think anyone read the Oz books any more; they were technologically out of date. He himself had read them, many times apiece, but that was years ago. "Do you like the Oz books?"

Donny nodded several times very fast. He thought about telling the man that he liked this one best, but was afraid to. Sometimes grownups laughed for no reason when he said he liked a book. Laughed and looked at him funny. They were probably thinking he should be outside playing football. But he decided to take a chance anyway. "This is my favorite Oz book. I've read it three times."

To Donny's relief, the man smiled. He hugged the book to his chest. "I gotta go now. My mother's over there." He motioned in the direction of the A & P across the street.

Martin nodded. He was delighted to have run into Donny, especially with an Oz book. He thought Ozma of Oz had disappeared along with Dr. Doolittle and Tom Swift and John Carter of Mars.

Donny was moving toward the door. Suddenly Martin called out, disregarding the fat librarian and the SILENCE sign on her desk. "My name is Martin, Donny."

Donny heard but he didn't turn around. He was glad the man told him his name but he didn't know what to answer. Just as he pushed open the door he heard the man say, "I used to love that book too."

And then he was jumping down the stone steps two at a time. This was something he had just learned and he was still practicing it. His mother was standing across the street by the Buick, looking like she was in a hurry. She was always in a hurry. They had to pick up his sister at Miss Petersen's, her tap-dance teacher.

Martin thought about the boy as he drove home. He suspected the boy didn't have many friends. If you had a lot of friends you didn't spend Saturday afternoon at Story Hour. There was Joe, of course, who'd hidden in the shrubbery, but he was younger. Besides, Donny had a solitary air. He couldn't say exactly why he thought this—not at first anyway. Then he remembered that he too had been solitary at that age, though he hadn't been able to figure out why until many years later. He simply didn't like to do what the other kids did, and that had separated him. But at Donny's age it had been a mystery. What he'd preferred to do, mostly, was to illustrate the stories he had read. He did this at the big desk where his mother wrote her letters. No one else seemed to appreciate this kind of activity, but it had led to his becoming an artist.

As Martin turned into his driveway, he wondered if he could do something to help the boy. He sighed. It would be difficult. The parents might not like it. He and Evan were, he suspected, the object of much gossip. Too much interest in a lonely child and the neighborhood mothers would call the sheriff.

Two days later he saw Donny riding past his house not once but four times, each time scanning the windows. On each pass he was followed by his enormous Great Dane, that looked just as eager and excited as he did. On the fourth ride past, Donny stopped and pretended to look at a squirrel on the lawn. Martin, who used the front room as a studio, watched all this. Although he knew he shouldn't, he got up and went to the front door. The boy's face lit up when he saw the door open and Martin could feel a frantic joy surge across the lawn toward him.

"Want a cup of hot chocolate, Donny?"

The boy nodded rapidly. It seemed to him that the most wonderful thing had happened. He walked his bike across the lawn. It left tire marks on patches of wet dirt. He was about to kick down the stand when the man spoke. "Maybe you better take it around back. I'll meet you there."

When Martin opened the back door, Donny and the dog were standing there, both quivering with excitement. "Frankie can wait outside," Donny said, patting the dog, whose tail was lashing back and forth like a whip.

It only took Martin a second to realize he didn't want the dog running around the yard advertising the boy's presence inside. "No, she can come on in."

He held the screen door open. Boy and dog bounded in. The dog was so big she could sweep the tops of the counters with her muzzle. Martin thought it was like having a pony in the house. "She likes to smell things," Donny advised, "but she won't eat anything except butter. We can't get her to stop licking butter."

"Well, there's no butter so she'll have to settle down."

While Donny made the dog lie in a corner he heated some water and emptied a packet of instant cocoa into a cup. He was very aware of the boy's presence. It seemed to change the kitchen—fill it up, charge the air. The boy had moved to the table of porcelainized zinc in the center of the room. He sat down, then put one elbow up and rested his head on his hand. He seemed very much at home. Martin recalled how he had always liked kitchens at that age, always been drawn to that part of the house. Whenever his grandmother would let him, he would mix ingredients picked from the shelf at random. Then he'd add water until he got a satisfactory, sludgy mess. He called this "cooking." He could only do it when his mother was out of the house—she said it was a waste of good food.

The boy began telling him that Frankie had had puppies last year. The father lived in a kennel and was a brindle. Three of the puppies had been brindle and four fawn. One of the fawns had died.

Donny felt very happy telling his new friend about the puppies. He usually found that grownups didn't listen. They preferred to correct him or interrupt. Sometimes, when he started to stammer, they made him slow down. This man didn't do any of those things. The idea that he had a new friend who would listen without correcting or interrupting was so thrilling that he thought of something important to ask him. A question so important and secret he hadn't even mentioned it to Joe White, who was eight and followed him around all the time.

The water was boiling. Martin poured it over the crumbled cocoa. Undissolved lumps floated to the top. "Better stir that, Donny." The boy got up on his knees so he could look directly into the cup. He stirred very carefully.

Martin could remember that position—on your knees on a kitchen chair. He wondered how many positions he had forgotten in the last thirty years. There was reading the funnies on the floor, for example, flat out on his stomach. He never did that any more.

The boy was having trouble lifting the cup. It was too full. Martin dashed over and held his wrist, which was still padded with fat, the carpus entirely buried. He had the sudden impression the boy was only an embryo, the merest blueprint of what he would become.

Donny finished the swallow and set down the cup. He ran his tongue over his lip, which was coated with chocolate. Frankie was hitting her tail against the linoleum. She had smelled the cocoa, he thought. Suddenly the man said to him, "Did you read that Oz book you had the other day?"

Donny stared. That was exactly what he wanted to ask about! Maybe the man could read his mind. He nodded. "That's my favorite one. I like it even better than *Glinda of Oz* or *Rinkitink in Oz*. My sister likes those best." He waited, watching. Would the man laugh? Sometimes, when he got too excited, people laughed. He never understood why. He had recently decided not to let people know he was excited.

But this man wasn't laughing. He was looking at him with nice crinkles around his caramel-colored eyes, which were the same color as his own.

"Why is that one your favorite?"

No one had ever asked him that before. Certainly not his mother, who disapproved of the Oz books because the school librarian, who he hated, had told her they were bad for children. He moved up on his knees again. He had to think and that helped. "Because of the list," he said at last.

"What list?"

Donny looked down at the cup of chocolate. He felt the way he did when the teacher called on him. Gummed-up inside. Still, he wanted to try. More than that, he wanted to ask his question.

Martin thought the boy was brimming with unsaid things. It suddenly struck him as quite sad. Where did this need to *tell* come from? Some days he couldn't wait for Evan to come home so he could tell him all the things that had happened—what birds had come to the feeder, what the plumber had said, how his ideas about a painting had changed. But in the act of telling it often became pointless. He would strain at meanings, struggle to find the exact word, and then stop. Evan's eye would be roving. He would clearly be thinking of something else— dinner, trouble at the office, a drink. What was the use? He had never been able to get across what he really felt, to clear out each day's accumulation of emotion. He wondered if the need to tell had arisen in a kitchen much like this, when he'd tried to tell someone about a book and they had refused to listen.

"The list that Randy has. He's the Purple Prince of Oz. His real name is Randywell Brandywell Brandenburg Bompadoo."

It took the boy a long time to get out the full title. He had to start over several times. Martin waited patiently.

"See, he has to do everything on the list so he can succeed to the throne. It's sort of a test."

Martin tried to remember. He recalled the cover of the book the boy had shown him in the library. A kid dressed in purple with some castles in the background. The Oz books were rather a blur. But then, suddenly, amazingly, he remembered. "Is that the one with the elephant?"

"Yes!" Donny screamed. "Kabumpo, the Elegant Elephant!"

He got so excited he knocked against the cup and it went over. Chocolate ran everywhere. Oh gosh, now he was going to get it. But to his surprise, the man didn't say anything. Just got a dishcloth and mopped it up. Then he asked if he wanted some more. Donny shook his head, no. He didn't have time to drink hot chocolate. He was getting too close to his question.

"So," Martin said, rinsing the dishcloth under the faucet, "there's a list of things the prince has to do to grow up."

"Not grow up, succeed to the throne, I told you." Why didn't the man pay attention? "When the King of Regalia dies his son has to go out on a journey. And do lots of things."

"I see. What kind of things?"

"All kinds!" Donny couldn't sit still any more. He got up and went over to Frankie, who started licking the chocolate from his fingers.

Martin observed the boy carefully. He was not a pretty child. His features were unbalanced—the forehead too narrow, the chin recessive, the eyes unfortunately close together. Some things would change but he wouldn't grow up to be a beauty. Suddenly his own mother's warning sounded in his ears: "You're not prepossessing, people don't like you when they meet you, but when they get to know you they appreciate your good qualities." A pain darted through him, the faintest replica of the first one.

"Can I ask you something?" Donny heard his own voice as if it were somebody else's. He'd never trusted anyone as much as he trusted this man. Was that wrong?

"Sure. Ask."

Martin saw that the boy was gasping again, his face contorted as he turned from the dog. He wondered if he was going to cry. Then he saw that the boy was just suffering from the weight of his unspoken thoughts.

"I was wondering. When you read the list. The list on the royal scroll. Did you think you had to do those things yourself?"

Martin closed his eyes. It was so long ago. So much had happened since then. Had he made a list of things to do? Had he taken a cue from Prince Randy? And then it came to him—the living room, the wing chair, the inlaid table next to it, the ashtray in the shape of a dragon. And the memory swept over him in a rush. "Yes I did. I did."

Donny found himself moving toward the man. It was coming now, the question he'd never been able to ask before. "Well, what I wanted to ask, did you do them? Did you do the things on Prince Randy's list?"

Martin stared into the boy's eyes. They seemed both young and old, foolish and wise. For a moment he had the impression he was looking into the well of life itself. So that was the question the boy had been carrying around with him. For how long?

"I don't really know, Donny. I haven't added it up." The boy had moved toward him and was now pressing against his knees. His body was soft and warm. Again Martin thought of an embryo, an unformed thing.

Donny wondered how to get the man to answer. It was terribly important. If the man would answer he would know what was going to happen to him for the rest of his life. "Could you try?"

Could he try? There had been so many people, so many comings and goings, so many changes. He shook his head. He was beginning to feel slightly impatient. "Maybe if you could bring the book over some time and read the list to me. Then I could tell you if I did all the things."

Donny was pressing against him harder. They seemed to be fusing into one person. The light had diminished in the kitchen—it was getting on toward evening. Pretty soon the kid's parents would wonder where he was. Shouldn't he put a stop to this?

"I know them by heart. There are six of them and I know them by heart."

"Oh my God, you know them by heart?"

Donny laughed. That was a curse. He liked to hear the man curse. "You want to hear them?"

Donny watched the man sit back, closing his eyes. He looked like he was getting smaller, younger. Maybe their talk had transformed the man, like magic. "First you have to make three true friends. Second, you have to serve a strange king. Third, you have to save a queen." He stopped to catch his breath. It was important to get them in the right order. "Then you have to prove your bravery in battle. Then you have to overcome a fabulous monster."

"Okay, hold on. I'm losing track."

But Donny didn't stop. There was only one left, his favorite. "And last," he said in a very loud voice, "you have to receive from a wizard some important treasure!"

Martin didn't reply when the boy finished. He was aware that his mind was racing, reviewing the past, trying to tally the score. But then he stopped himself. This was silly. You didn't keep score in life, not if you were smart.

"Gee, Donny, I can't tell you what I did. It happened too long ago."

He could see that this upset the boy. "Try!" Donny jiggled up and down. His eyes were glistening and there was spit at the corners of his mouth. Martin thought that the boy's life would be very hard unless he stopped caring so much. "You have to try!"

The command seemed to resonate in his chest, chiming old things into life. He sat back, closing his eyes. How many items on the list had he fulfilled?

The first was friends. Certainly he'd made three true friends—more than that. He had been gifted at friendship; it was one of the things he had discovered quite early. No problem there.

Serving a strange king. He had never much liked taking orders. How many situations had he walked out on, simply because he despised any display of power? He had also detested deans, top sergeants, bosses and cops. And yet . . . hadn't there been someone? The answer came in the shape of Lincoln's dark torso, now gleaming again in blue-black perfection. He'd met Lincoln at a bar on the waterfront—a place that had taken him weeks of self-priming in order to visit. It had been filled with the most dangerous-looking men he'd ever seen. And Lincoln had seemed the most dangerous of all—a man so rare, so exotic that he seemed to sum up every impulse Martin had ever forbidden himself. But he had surrendered. That night and many nights after, until Lincoln, and what they did, was no longer rare or exotic but simply another road to physical satisfaction. And out of that he had learned something important—not to be afraid, not to draw back. Lincoln had been not a strange king but a king of strangeness. After that brief period of service Martin had never been afraid of his own desires again.

He opened his eyes. Donny was staring at him. His restlessness of a few minutes before was gone; he seemed to be taking nourishment from Martin's silence. Was it possible he could read his thoughts? He closed his eyes again.

Saving a queen. There had been a great many in his life, all self-crowned, but none so royal as Eda Goodwin. A widow when he met her, in her late fifties, they had slammed together like freight cars and hooked up in devotion and mutual aid for twenty years, until her death. She was lonely, reckless, unable to cope with solitude. He had squired her around, looked after her investments, helped her in a thousand little ways. And when she went on one of her drunks, which were not infrequent, he had made sure she got home in safe company. She was, he had often thought, the very opposite of his own mother — in fact, he had come to think of her as the un-mother, the anti-mother, who had untied in him all the knots slipped on by the original. He had saved her, yes — but she had also saved him. It had been one of those odd, succoring relationships that fit no mold. He still missed her.

"Are you thinking?"

Martin smiled and rubbed the boy's cheek. "Yeah, I've been thinking."

"Did you do the things?"

"Well, I guess I've had three friends and served a king and saved a queen."

Donny peered at him but didn't ask for details. "What about the rest?"

Martin's mind circled back. *You have to prove your bravery in battle.* Hadn't he done that with Evan, in the years they had been together? Faced hatred from relatives, employers, neighbors? Struggled to keep their self-respect in a world deadset on depriving them of it? Wasn't that bravery of the dreary, everyday kind that was tougher than a cavalry charge or a firefight? And the fabulous monster. There had been a lot of those, but none more monstrous or fabulous than his father. He could still see the ogre of his childhood, with wire-rimmed glasses and a paunch. But he had subdued the ogre. Done so the day he'd come home for a visit and found his father tossing lighted fire-crackers at their old and trembling dog — who was almost as big as this one — while laughing through his yellow rotted teeth. He had knocked the man down. And even as he knocked him down for his meanness and sadism he had knocked down his own guilt and fear. Did all that count?

"Did you think of the next two?"

"Yeah, Donny, I did. There wasn't one battle, there were lots of them. But I never ran away. And the monster—I guess I won that one too, in a way."

Donny pressed closer in. Martin could feel the soft flesh, the buried bones. A boy-blob with dirty hands. But he smelled good, like freshly turned earth or a risen loaf.

"There's one more," Donny said firmly. He liked the feel of the man's legs trapping his own. He thought that even if he struggled the man wouldn't let him go. Ever.

"What's that one? I've forgotten."

"Oh!" Donny was exasperated. How could the man forget the most important one? "You have to get some magic from a wizard!"

"Oh yes." Martin pinched the place where his nose met his forehead. Wizards weren't exactly his line. Still, he had dabbled in Zen, Yoga, various sects and cults, including primalism, shamanism, vegetarianism and the Great Goddess. He had met a great many sages and sorcerers, men and women who gave him truths to store in the drying chambers of his mind, bits of wisdom so fragile they could blow away in a breeze and so strong they could last a thousand years. Still, none of that seemed to fit the bill exactly.

Donny was pounding on his knee now. He was obviously getting bored. Maybe it was time to stop this game and send him home. Besides, Evan would be arriving any minute. He would, Martin knew, disapprove strongly if he found the boy on the premises. They had agreed to keep him away.

"Well how about it?"

"Quit that, it hurts."

"Then tell me about the wizard!"

The boy's command decayed slowly in the darkening air and then, quite clearly, Martin understood. Life itself was the wizard—it had taught him everything he needed to know, at exactly the time he needed it. The spells, the salves, the genie lamps had all come to hand. He had been surrounded by wizardry without even knowing it. Could he explain this to the boy? And then, looking at his eager face, he knew he didn't have to. All he had to impart was his confidence; anything more was unnecessary. The boy stared at him, motionless, as if soaking all this in. Then he broke away. "I gotta go," he said.

Martin got up and led him to the door. The dog came along, first yawning and stretching. Martin watched the boy kick the stand out from under his bike, then wheel it out of sight. He felt suddenly exhausted. The conversation had drained him in unsuspected ways.

Just as Donny got to the front he saw the other man's car head into the driveway. This man looked at him in an angry way but Donny didn't care. This wasn't his friend anyway. He didn't even give him a wave. On the street, Donny got aboard his bike using his one-foot flying mount. He knew he did this extremely well. He wished the first man had been around to see it.

When Martin saw Evan enter the house he went over and gave him a hug. Evan smelled grimy and citified, not at all like the boy. "Busy day?"

"You bet." Evan looked grim. "I see you had company."

"Yeah. He dropped by." Martin said some other things, mostly reassuring, but Evan didn't seem convinced. Martin finally decided to change the subject and started to talk about Prince Randywell and his list. But a minute later he felt the old strain, the difficulty of conveying exactly what he felt. "I found out . . ." but the words dissolved in the corridors of his brain and he gave an embarrassed laugh. Why bother? But a moment later he tried again. "I found out that when the king dies in the kingdom of Regalia his son has to go out and prove his fitness to receive the crown. It's written on the royal scroll."

Evan was staring at him. "Good God, Martin."

He gave another feeble laugh. "Well, it's true."

Evan was peeling off his tie and shirt. In another minute he'd go upstairs and change his clothes. "Have you thought about getting a parttime job? Maybe you're alone in this place too much. It isn't healthy." Then, without waiting for an answer, he left the room.

Martin remained alone, suddenly depressed. Why had he tried? Why didn't he keep his mouth shut? What was the source of his idiotic desire to make people understand? He remained standing, quite still, until Evan returned. He didn't refer to his time with Donny again, and now the words came quite easily.

When Donny got home his mother was annoyed. But he didn't tell her where he'd been. His friendship with the man was a secret. He couldn't talk about it. If he did, he'd get excited and stammer and they'd make fun of him. His father came home a while later. Donny didn't say much until his father kicked Frankie for lying in front of his chair. Then he tried to hit his father. But his father just laughed and held his arms and then he was sent to bed early.

The Purple Prince

Alone in his room, Donny looked at himself in the mirror over the bookcase. On top of the bookcase was a stuffed baby alligator with a light bulb in its mouth. His grandmother had sent it from Florida last year. It was his favorite possession. After thinking for a moment, he plugged in the cord that came out of the alligator's behind. The red light went on, giving him a fiendish look in the mirror. He started making faces. He loved contorting his features like this; it made him new and mysterious.

At the same moment, Martin was standing in his bathroom, observing himself in the light of bulbs spaced around the mirror. It was a stagey light, quite harsh. It showed lines he didn't usually see.

And then, oddly enough, the two friends were able to see each other even though they were miles apart. This is because a mirror is also a kind of window. Donny stopped making fiendish faces in the red glow and Martin stopped examining the deep lines around his eyes. Instead, they looked at each other. When they did, both pairs of eyes widened, as if they were camera lenses expanding to admit the faintest gleams of light. And then, as they stared, they saw that although they were suspended between two worlds, one looking into the future and one into the past, they were really as one. In the next instant both smiled and waved. There was nothing to be afraid of. The tests ahead and behind were fitted to the measure of their lives as gloves are fitted to the hand — nothing extra, nothing short — and this was exactly the way it should be. In fact, it had been arranged from the very beginning.

They looked at each other for another minute or two, this time without smiling, and then the window, or mirror, closed down. As each settled into bed for the night he thought that it had been a most remarkable day, thanks to the Purple Prince of Oz.

The Night Visitors

For two nights in a row, the car had pulled up in their driveway. The first night, Jack thought someone just wanted to turn around, but when he saw the three men staring at the house, he went to the window. Not that he could see much — just three bulky shapes, two in the front, one in the back. But when the headlights cut off, and the car sat in the dark, he felt a brief stab in the pit of his stomach. It seemed the beginning of a drama that had begun a long time ago — in a dream, or in his childhood.

The car had stayed three, maybe four minutes. Then the driver tooted the horn, turned on the lights and backed out. The sound of the horn had seemed harsh and derisive to Jack, almost as if it might be unscrambled into words and sentences. It rang in his ears for a long time, adding an unpleasant undertone to the music Rudi was playing on the stereo. Rudi always played music in the evening. Tonight he was sewing muslin backing on drapes, moving his hands quickly as he hummed snatches of *Falstaff*. He had not heard the horn and Jack said nothing. He knew what Rudi's reaction would be — widened eyes, a hand pressed to his neck and a bad night. Better keep it to himself.

But the car returned the next night, just at bedtime. They were already upstairs. The crocheted bedspread had been folded, the blanket switched on. He heard the crunch of wheels on gravel and realized he had been listening for it all evening, listening as one might listen for a knock on the door in Hitler Germany. He had a sudden dizzy sense that he had willed the intrusion through some error or malfeasance of his own, some deed not done or done too late — and that the car had arrived in retribution. For a few moments he wondered at his capacity for guilt, then put the whole question out of his mind. The situation had to be dealt with on a reality level. Phantoms were only the forms of self-indulgence.

Rudi, coming out of the bathroom, saw him standing at the window. He moved to his side and Jack smelled his familiar odor—freshly crushed leaves mixed with Habit Rouge. "What is it?" Rudi asked.

"Nothing."

Jack glanced at him. Rudi's eyebrows had formed little gothic arches over his grey eyes. "Why are you standing there?"

Keeping his voice level, Jack replied, "It's a car. They came by last night too." Still offhand, he added. "Turn off the light."

He hadn't fooled Rudi. "I knew it," he said. "I knew it."

Jack felt a rush of annoyance. "Oh for Christ's sake."

They stood in the dark for several minutes. It seemed very unreal to Jack, as if they were playing hide-and-seek and he and Rudi had chosen to conceal themselves in a vacant house.

"He-e-e-e-ey-y-y!"

The words rolled toward the house in a shrill wave.

A pause, then a different voice. "We know you're in there, boys."

They waited. At last the car lights went on—two thick torches illuminating the shrubs on the lawn. With an arrogant blast of the horn, the car sprang into life and roared away.

They stood for a long time without speaking. In fact, neither spoke until they were in bed. Perhaps it was the safety of the four-poster or the familiarity of that touch—hip against hip, leg against leg—that released them.

"I think we should call the police." Rudi's breath was warm in his ear.

"They haven't done anything yet."

Rudi murmured something but Jack didn't listen. His thoughts were circling back to the events that had led them here to Belle Terre, studying them to see where the error had begun. There had been the house-hunting with the agent, a heavy woman who had insisted on being called Eleanor. She had been born here in the upper Catskills but had lived in New York City for many years. She told them this, Jack realized, to stress her familiarity with all kinds of unusual people. After the closing she had offered to introduce them to two men who had bought a house in the next county.

There had been Walter Jensen, the farmer whose place they had bought. He had studied them with eyes cold as asteroids, then asked if either of them had ever handled a chain saw. There had been Mr.

Jencks, the mortgage officer at the bank, who had taken a dislike to
Rudi, refusing to look at him or address him. At the signing he had
handed Rudi the pen without a word.

Now, lying in bed, Jack wondered if any of these might have been
clues he had overlooked, clues to the fact that they were daring too
much. *Hubris*. The word came to him as he visualized their names on
the deed—Rudolph Berczy and John E. Birnbaum. Was it hubris that
had led them to chuck their jobs in the city and embark on a wholesale
nursery operation in the mountains? Hubris that had led them to
believe they would be welcomed by the people of the town—or at least
accepted? Hubris that had led them to get drunk on champagne on
their first night in this house—a drunkenness that had led them
straight upstairs to bed, where he had cradled Rudi's bald head and
tracked his long bones under the white skin until he felt lust and joy
course through him in such amounts he thought his skin would pop?

Rudi rolled over, probably annoyed because he hadn't continued
the conversation, but Jack paid no attention. Another image had
come to him—the image of seven fat cows and seven lean ones. He
and Rudi had had seven fat years together and now there was famine
ahead. Staring into the dark, aware of his friend's uneven breathing,
it struck Jack that he had access to any number of mythologies, but
that none of them really applied to their present situation. Maybe
Rudi had been right. Maybe they should call the police.

They didn't speak much the next morning. Jack recognized the
signs of anxiety. For one thing, he had trouble with numbers, making
careless errors in his calculations for the greenhouse foundation. Several times he tilted the wheelbarrow badly and dumped his load of
concrete blocks. But behind the buzzing in his head was something
else, something pulling him toward a place he didn't want to go. In
that place music was being played—the theme music for "Let's Pretend." "Let's Pretend" had been his favorite radio show as a child, a
half hour of dramatized fairy tales transporting him from the cramped
Brooklyn apartment, away from his father, totally blind, who gave
endless piano lessons to mediocre students in the dining room. The
theme music had been the entrance to another world—one so perfect
that when the half hour was over he felt angry and cheated for the rest
of the day.

Now, when the theme music became almost deafening, he stopped
work and stalked to a rock at the bottom of the yard. There he sat

tensely and smoked several cigarettes.

They didn't talk much at lunch. Jack knew that his anxiety had communicated itself to Rudi, who was usually very cheerful at meal-times. Today Rudy said hardly anything except "Stop jiggling." Jack hadn't realized he was twitching his leg. It was a nervous habit.

The morning mail had brought some seed catalogs and a letter from his mother, which he read and passed on to Rudi. To his surprise his friend threw it down and snapped, "She doesn't even know I'm alive."

Jack looked at him surprise. His mother never sent her regards to Rudi, never acknowledged that her precious son shared his life. But his mother's obstinacy had always amused Rudi—at least until now. Jack watched him move around the kitchen—his slender frame rigid with anger—and wondered if he should apologize. He decided against it. His mother wasn't the real cause of Rudi's bad temper. He let his thoughts touch lightly on the night visitors again. Actually, there were a number of explanations he hadn't yet considered. The three men had lost their way. They were having car trouble. They wanted to use the phone. But even as he accepted the faint comfort of these thoughts, his stomach gave a sour lurch. He was pretending again. His eye fell on the letter. Perhaps pretending ran in the Birnbaum family.

He recalled his mother's initial visit to the apartment he and Rudi had first shared—a walkup on Second Avenue. She had inspected the furniture, the kitchen, the twin beds, the carefully chosen plants and pictures. She was a small wiry woman with black walnut eyes and the trace of an accent. She had been born in Odessa. When she didn't get her way she seemed to grow harder and more wiry—almost to shrivel into a hard kernel of mulishness while her eyes glittered. Now, after touring the apartment, Jack could see her body tense, her face grow rigid. "I wish," she had hissed, and he had steeled himself for her words, "I wish . . . I could burn every stick of furniture in this place." And then, unaccountably, she had smiled at him, as if to wipe out the words, the ugly words that dismissed everything he and Rudi had worked to achieve—indeed, denied their whole life together. Her black eyes, luminous with mother-love, had searched his face, testing his reaction, his loyalties. And then he had done a strange thing. He had pretended not to hear! He had pretended she had not spoken! He had actually smiled and talked of something else.

The knowledge hammered at him now, at the table holding her letter—the knowledge that he had refused to defend his life with Rudi. From that refusal had flowered others—her persistent snubbing of Rudi, her belief that he himself would eventually marry a nice girl from the neighborhood, her statement that he was only going through a phase.

A phase! He shook his head. Some phase. He had just turned forty. He hoisted himself from the table. Rudi was at the sink, staring through the window at the herb garden. "We shouldn't have come here," he said without turning around.

"What kind of horseshit is that?" Jack was surprised at the anger in his voice, surprised at the way his heavy body trembled. "Three months here and you're ready to give up? Because somebody drives in our driveway?"

Rudi turned to look at him, his face full of pain, but Jack was not appeased. He felt like giving Rudi a good shake, a shake that would make his teeth rattle and his bones jangle. But just as suddenly his anger turned to despair. It was not Rudi but his mother whom he wanted to shake—his mother sitting there and looking at him with black walnut eyes, inviting him to join her in the family game of "Let's Pretend."

They didn't make up until they were driving to town in midafternoon. Jack reached over and touched Rudi's knee. "I don't know what we were all steamed up about," he said.

Rudy's sinewy hand rested on his for a moment. "It'll be okay," he replied. Jack could feel the determination flow between them. It was strange. Their strengths seemed to alternate and overlap. As Rudi parked the car he reflected that they had simply been afflicted with newcomer nerves. It was silly to imagine they could transplant themselves without making a few waves. It was to be expected. They had been left unprepared—victimized, really—by their own complacency.

Feeling better than he had all day, he went into the hardware store. Rudi stayed in the car. The youngest clerk, who was named Jimmy and was just out of high school, came over. He was a breezy young man with the remains of a bad case of acne.

"I saw you and your friend over to the Saugerties auction," Jimmy said, "you guys thinkin' of buyin' yourself some horses?" Jimmy's voice was light and pleasant. A country voice saying country things. But it had an odd effect on Jack. His right arm jerked and a buzzing started in his ears. Suddenly, fearfully, it occurred to him that Jimmy might be one of the three men in the car. His eyes ran down the youth's figure, trying to fit it into one of the bulky forms he remembered. Was it possible? Possible that he wasn't Jimmy from the hardware but a nightrider, a phobic figure out to destroy their new life? His heart started to pound, even as he knew he had to fight this absurd notion. It was his turn to say something now, to toss off some light remark about horses and girlfriends. But he couldn't. Jimmy was looking at him in a puzzled way and he tried again to say the word that would signify all was well. But in the deepest, oldest part of his mind, he could feel accusations taking hold, wrongs being dusted off. He turned quickly and headed for the door, aware of Jimmy's alarmed expression, sick with the thought that he was acting like an idiot. Only by a special effort was he able to turn at the door and mutter something about coming back later.

As they drove toward the Grand Union, Jimmy's words echoed in his head. *You and your friend. You and your friend.* Suddenly they were accompanied, underscored, by the theme music to "Let's Pretend." It seemed an absurd pairing, and he tried to separate them, but without success. By the time Rudi had nosed the car into the parking lot and switched off the engine, Jack's head was awash with echoes. He had to wait a few moments, getting control of himself, before he could follow Rudi into the store.

As they made their way down the aisles, the cart rattling under his hand, Jack found his head clearing but a vast impatience occupying him. Rudi liked to shop carefully, to read the unit prices, do sums in his head. Several times Jack was on the point of yelling at him, but managed to reduce his words to a growl. Rudi was not to be rushed, however. He moved slowly, his half-glasses on his nose, reading the labels. When they reached the meat counter, Rudi pawed over the roasts, then rang the bell. "What are you doing?" Jack hissed, but Rudi looked at him blandly and didn't reply. The window behind the counter slid open and the butcher leaned out, a blond man with a smooth veal-like face. The butcher gave a friendly nod. "Hello, Mr. Berczy," he said. He pronounced it correctly. Jack blinked rapidly. Where had the butcher learned Rudi's name?

"Max, how are you today?" Rudi was smiling intimately. Jack realized, in a gust of horror, that Rudi was actually flirting with the butcher. "Don't you have anything nicer than this for me today?"

Rudi held up the hunk of beef and pointed with disgust to the fatty side. He might have been displaying a diseased hand or arm. The butcher took the roast. "Guess we should have trimmed it a bit." He left the window. Jack could see him inside, looking through a tray of carcasses. Rudi turned to Jack with a blissful air. "Max always does something special for me," he announced.

Some other shoppers were observing them. Jack saw several young women with children, smiling and trading glances. Their little negotiation with Max was obviously amusing them. He turned back to find Rudi glaring at him. "What's the matter with you?"

Jack shook his head. 'Nothing."

"Jesus Christ, you certainly don't act like it." Rudi was furious, Jack could see. The scarlet vein on his forehead stood out. His shopping had been ruined.

Max was at the window again. "Here you go, Mr. Berczy."

Rudi took the package and put it in the cart. They started off, Rudi maintaining an injured silence. Several times Jack started to explain, then checked himself. What was there to explain? How could he tell Rudi about Jimmy in the hardware store and his sudden terror? Rudi wouldn't understand. Rudi was much simpler than he was, his mind less cluttered. It was Rudi's directness that had drawn them together in the first place.

With a sudden sense of loss, Jack thought that he and Rudi were worlds apart, in spite of everything.

That night, after the dinner dishes were done, Rudi took out his curtain backing and began to sew. They had given each other a wide berth for the rest of the day. Speaking little, attending to the necessary tasks, waiting until the little scene at the Grand Union had sorted itself out, been absorbed into their bodies the way a pimple or a bruise is absorbed. He himself had calmed down when they reached home, felt better, even had a brief nap. Now, sitting in the Boston rocker reading *Horticulture*, he reflected that by tomorrow morning, with the new day and fresh birdsong, this day's hazard would be forgotten. Erased by the benediction of sleep. He let his gaze rove around the living room with its hooked rug and converted kerosene lamps and pine chest. What could happen in their own home? Weren't they masters here? Wasn't it safe from infection? A sudden optimism swept through him. There wouldn't be any mysterious car tonight.

The visitors had given up, discouraged by the lack of response. He settled back in the rocker and read an ad for an all-plastic greenhouse. He wondered if it would be safe from woodchucks. He had already shot twelve woodchucks with his new .22, but there seemed to be an endless supply.

He was deep in an article on greenhouse sprinkling systems when the sound from outside pierced his concentration. His body stirred even before his mind identified the sound. The evening, he noticed, was just going into its final dark. It would be nine o'clock. Rudi had frozen, his needle in the air. With an odd feeling, as if this action had occurred before and had been stored, ready for use, for countless ages, Jack stood up, put the magazine in the brass kettle that served as a rack and moved toward the front door. As he turned the knob, he had a sudden absurd image of his mother. She was standing at his side and her eyes were glinting with victory. *See*, she croaked, *this is what you get.*

He opened the door and stepped out on the little concrete stoop.

The driver of the car was the first to emerge. He was a man in his late twenties wearing olive fatigues with bulging side pockets. He was tall but his body seemed slack. He looked at Jack in a friendly way and nodded, "Hiya doin?"

"Okay," said Jack, surprised at the false cheer in his voice.

The man came a few paces closer, then stopped. "Thought we'd stop by and see how you was gettin' along." He seemed nervous standing there in the fading light. He hooked one thumb in his belt. "My friend," he jerked his head toward the car, "needs to take a piss." He laughed hollowly and turned his head sideways, looking at Jack as a bird might.

Take a piss. Jack weighed the information in his mind. It seemed to have something wrong about it—not quite fit into the mountain twilight and the darkening upland on which they stood. But he didn't care to explore it further. Besides, the occupant of the rear seat had gotten out. He was a short, powerful man in khakis and a red flannel shirt. He was nodding in a friendly way that seemed to require a greeting. "How are you?" Jack said.

"Tell them to go away." Rudi's voice was in his ear. He was standing in the doorframe, his body arched like a bow.

"That there's Matt," said the first man. "My name's Eldred."

He stepped forward and put out his hand. It seemed impossible not to take it. Jack introduced himself, then Rudi. Rudi nodded curtly, keeping his hands at his side. The two visitors did not seem offended.

"Gotta go so bad I can taste it," Matt smiled. Jack could see he had a squint in one eye, giving him a strangely innocent look. "Iff'n you don't mind," Matt added.

Again, Jack knew there was something wrong to all this, and again he turned away from the realization. In the next instant he was annoyed at his suspicions. Why should he assume the worst about this visit? Why should he ascribe hostile intentions to these two men?

They were both standing in his yard, shuffling their feet, waiting for an invitation. An invitation inside. Wasn't that the country way of doing things? Inviting your neighbors into the house when they came to call? This wasn't New York City, where you slammed the door in people's faces.

With a sudden expansive gesture, he motioned to the house. "Come on in," he said. He heard Rudi's sharp breath but paid no attention. "What about your friend?" He nodded toward the car.

"Oh Alvin," Eldred replied, smiling, "he ain't interested in nothin' much."

Rudi stepped aside at the last minute and the two men filed in, looking around quickly. "Bathroom's upstairs," Jack said to Matt.

Matt went upstairs, his heavy tread shaking the stairs. Jack led Eldred into the living room. "You done a good job," Eldred said as he settled into the Boston rocker without being asked. Jack wondered if he had known the previous owner.

"We've been working on it for three months."

"So I hear."

"You guys thirsty?" The words had slipped out without his willing them. Rudi, by the front door, coughed warningly.

"Sure are," Eldred replied. Jack could see that his eyes were light blue and his teeth small and yellow.

"How about a beer?"

"Sure thing."

When he returned with the beers, Rudi refusing to stir, Matt was coming down the stairs. Jack, with the tray, followed him into the living room.

"Sure took you a long time," Eldred said to Matt, "what was you doin', shakin' it dry?"

Matt let out a guffaw and squinted at Jack in a hangdog way. Then he stroked his crotch lightly—once, twice—and muttered, "Guess so."

Watching this, Jack felt curiously weightless. For an instant he had the impression that these men had taken over and he was a guest in his own house. "Cheers," he said, lifting his beer.

They drank up. Eldred sighed when he finished and wiped his mouth.

"You guys live around here?" Once again Jack felt that the words had come out of their own accord.

"Down to Fleischmanns," Eldred replied affably. "Matt's in the parts business."

"Oh? What kind of parts?"

"Auto. Tractor," Matt mumbled.

Jack nodded but could think of nothing further to say. When he didn't speak, the visitors shifted position. Eldred hunched forward on the rocker, Matt on the pine chest. It occurred to Jack that they would soon finish their beers and leave.

The silence lengthened. Then, out of the corner of his eye, Jack saw Matt's hand move toward his crotch. The weightlessness assailed him again.

"We're starting a wholesale nursery operation," he said quickly and loudly. The hand stopped. "You know, poinsettias at Christmas, lilies at Easter . . ." The two men looked at him. "We expect to go into it in a pretty big way."

Neither replied. He saw Matt's hand start toward his crotch again.

"We might be able to give you two some work if you want it." Once again the words had tumbled out of their own accord.

"Jack!" It was Rudi, the first time he had spoken. They looked at him. His eyes were huge. "We don't know what we're going to need."

Why was Rudi contradicting him? Was he trying to make him look like a fool? "I know that. I'm just saying . . ."

"It's too soon to say *anything*."

Eldred nodded sympathetically. "Sure. You're just gettin' started."

"Right," Matt echoed from the corner. Jack could see that his hand was nailed to his crotch, bunching his genitals. Then he saw the two visitors glance at each other. Eldred moved his tongue across his lips. Jack had the impression of great delicacy. And then he knew that the moment had come. Several sentences took shape in his mind. "You guys got the wrong idea." "I don't know why you came here but . . ."

But even as he fashioned the words, his mind refused to agree. Nothing had happened. Nothing would happen. These people were his friends.

"People in town is talkin' about you two. They says you suck dick real good." The tone was mild and the words were followed by a little laugh.

For a moment Jack wasn't sure where the words had come from. From the stereo? From the china dog by the fireplace?

No, they had come from Eldred, who was now leering at him in an embarrassed way. The room became still. Everything seemed to slide away and, amazingly, Jack became aware of his mother's presence again. She was looking at him vindictively. *You see?* she said. *You see?*

Although he knew what his mother meant, at the same time he thought she didn't understand. Not about Rudi and saving their money and their first night upstairs and the greenhouse and . . . well, the rest of their lives.

And something else. What could that be?

The silence lengthened. Jack realized the visitors were as nervous as he was. There were several things he could do. But first he had to find out what that something else was. It seemed quite important to their future in Belle Terre.

"Well," his voice again, "it's good to know what people are saying about you."

The visitors twisted on their seats.

"We don't give a shit." It was Rudi, his face ugly with anger. He had moved to the fireplace. Jack saw him glance down at the poker. In another moment, Jack knew, Rudi would grab it and start swinging. He had to prevent that.

And then Jack realized that what he had to find out had nothing to do with Rudi either. The words of Jimmy in the hardware tolled faintly in his ears. *You and your friend.* Yes, Jimmy thought of them as a pair, a couple. And if Jimmy did then others did too—everyone in Belle Terre, in fact. And then Jack saw that he had been walking around town for three months in a magic cloak—a cloak that rendered his relationship with Rudi invisible.

He watched Eldred's tongue flicker across his lips. In a moment he would have to act. But first he wanted to place the magic cloak. Of course. It had been on "Let's Pretend." And then, in a last burst of clear-sightedness, he saw that the cloak was the cause of the trouble tonight. Safe in its folds, its enchantment, he had refused to see.

He stood up quickly. Matt and Eldred stared at him warily, but didn't try to stop him when he walked out. As he got the gun from the closet in the kitchen, it occurred to him that the two men were not dangerous, merely ignorant.

It only took a moment to slip in the shells. When he got back, the gun across his chest, the visitors were standing up.

"You can put that thing down." It was Matt. His deep voice sounded almost dignified.

"Get out." Jack pointed the gun toward the door.

The two men looked at each other, then Eldred, showing his small yellow teeth, said, "No offense."

"No, no offense." He waved the gun again.

The two men filed out. Rudi trailed at a distance, a low furious hum coming out of his throat. When the visitors were halfway down the flagstone walk, Eldred turned around and spat. "Faggots," he said.

"Fuck you," Rudi screamed. Jack could see his jugular standing out like a drainpipe. He motioned to Rudi.

They waited on the stoop as the visitors got in their car. Eldred, after starting up, swerved suddenly to mow down a line of rhododendrons they had just planted, then veered back. He spat once more through the side-window before driving off.

They waited on the stoop for several minutes, not speaking as they waited to calm down. Jack had the sudden sense that the yard, the house, even the unfinished greenhouse, now belonged to them in a new way, as if these things were both simpler and more real.

It also occurred to him that there might be further trouble with the night visitors. They might come back with some friends. At the same time, he felt confident. He would leave the gun by the front door, the shells handy. He would also alert the sheriff.

"Those bastards. I wish you'd shot 'em."

"Next time I will. It would be a pleasure." He shivered suddenly, although the evening was quite warm. The next moment he saw that his mother, wearing her most mulish expression, had materialized at his side in a stream of cold air. *Hello ma*, he whispered under his breath, not wanting Rudi to hear, *hello*. And then he saw quite clearly what he had to do.

"I'm going to call New York."

Rudi stared at him. "Whatever for?"

"I want to talk to ma."

"About what happened?"

"No. About something else."

Rudi was still watching him, eyebrows pointing, but Jack didn't bother to explain. There would be plenty of time for that.

With a last look around they turned and entered the house. While Rudi removed the beer cans from the living room, Jack punched out the numbers on the phone. When his mother answered, with her usual breathlessness, he began to speak slowly and evenly. He told her about the new house, the new furniture and the new business. He spoke of Rudi's contribution to all this and about their plans for the future. During this long recital he did not allow her to interrupt, not once. When he finished he hung up gently and sat by the phone without twitching or jiggling. Then he got up and headed for the kitchen. On the way he wondered if he didn't owe a debt—a very tiny debt—to the night visitors.

The Piano

He shouldn't have accepted the invitation. He didn't belong in this richly-furnished apartment, with its original Barcelona chairs, its coffee table of thick glass, its antique Bodhisattva and Bokhara rug. That was his first mistake. His second was to sit down at the piano. He'd tried to resist, of course, but it hadn't worked for very long. The instrument in the center of the room—its curved flank gleaming, its keyboard bared like the teeth of some splendid beast—had eventually lured him to it.

"Why don't you play something, Phil?" Klaus had said—or rather, commanded—soon after he entered. But he had shaken his head quickly, nervously, and headed for one of the Barcelona chairs. Not, unfortunately, before he'd reached out in passing and brushed that silken flank, registered the sensuality of it all, the way the instrument seemed to quiver with the burden of unreleased song.

Klaus had watched with narrowed eyes and a mirthless smile. But, safe in the Barcelona chair, Phil resolved again not to play. Touching the piano was like an appetite that had to be kept under control. There was no telling where it might lead him.

"I am fixing drinks," Klaus said in his clipped, authoritative way, then headed into the kitchen. He didn't ask what Phil wanted. Again the feeling came over him that he didn't belong here. A condominium on Fifth Avenue was too far from his own messy studio on Bleecker Street. Klaus Ohmann was too remote from his own situation.

They'd met at a party a few weeks before, a party where many of the guests wore pants of soft leather or a tiny diamond in one ear or skintight shirts through which could be seen the outline of a nipple ring. At one point in the evening capsules of chemicals had been passed around on silver trays; later a montage of Pepsi commercials

had been projected on a high wall. Phil knew the host only slightly—
an alcoholic who issued invitations to his parties as if they were
subpoenas.

The small round man with dyed lemon hair and bright blue eyes
had found Phil standing alone beside a floor lamp. "I don't come to
parties like this often," the stranger had said, snapping off the syllables.
He had a slight German accent, not displeasing. Phil had the impression that he knew things about the English language—its trapdoors
and hinges—that he himself had never discovered. "I do not dress in
the bohemian way."

It was true. The man, who was about fifty, was wearing a three-
piece suit with a silk tie. The gold frames of his spectacles matched
the gold of his hair, his cuff links and watch. He stood very close to
Phil so that his right arm brushed him occasionally. To avoid this,
Phil moved backward until he was barricaded in a corner.

The man, who introduced himself as Klaus, had been in the United
States for twenty years. Before that he had worked in Frankfurt and
London. He was attached to a big international bank. He did not tell
Phil which one. "Now tell me what you do, please," Klaus said when
his brief resumé ended.

Phil was irked by the question but managed to smile. He really
didn't like to put his life into a tidy package. There were too many—
well, loose ends. Still, he decided that friendliness was behind the
question and he might as well answer. He told Klaus, in his soft voice,
that he was from a coal-mining area in western Pennsylvania, that he
had studied music at Indiana and later gotten a master's in piano at
Juilliard.

"So you are a pianist!" Klaus seemed very excited by this news. His
blue eyes blazed and he squeezed Phil's upper arm tightly. Feeling
even more beleaguered, Phil murmured that he'd given up music
about a year ago. Now he worked for a credit-card company. He was
hoping to get into their computer department.

He didn't tell Klaus the real reason why he had given up music.
The fact was, he found he hated the kind of concert career for which
he had trained. He didn't like the rudeness and egotism, the bad
hotels and cold rehearsal halls, the impersonality of the impresarios
and the spitefulness of the critics. He knew his reaction to the musical marketplace wasn't admirable—you were supposed to rise above
it through strength of character—but he couldn't help it. He hadn't

been made for all that, and besides, it had nothing to do with music. After two mini-tours, mostly to college towns, he had told his agent he was quitting.

The fact that he had given up music didn't seem to bother Klaus, however. In fact, he pushed in a little closer. "You are a pianist, even though you are not playing now." A soundless laugh formed on his lips. "You are young, you will perhaps change your mind."

"You can't be a pianist if you don't play. I sold my piano."

"Why?"

"If it was in the apartment I'd practice every spare minute. I'd never have time for anything else."

Klaus Ohmann laughed mirthlessly again. "Then you must come to my house and try my piano. I have a Steinway, it is waiting for you."

Before leaving the party Phil had, with some misgiving, written out his home phone for Klaus. It rang two evenings later. Could Phil come for dinner? It would be a great honor to have a musician in the house.

Klaus emerged from the kitchen with two glasses, frosty and multicolored. "Campari and bitter lemon," he said, thrusting one at Phil, "excellent for the warm weather." He sat on the Barcelona chair alongside Phil's, then raised his glass in a toast. Phil followed suit. The drink was not unpleasant.

Phil was just wondering how he'd get through the long evening when, as if he'd read his mind, Klaus said, "You know we are having another guest?" He motioned toward the dining table. Three places were set. "He is a doctor. A fine tenor. Perhaps he will sing for us."

Phil sat back, relieved. It would be easier with a third party around. Klaus' pudgy hands had already landed on his arm several times. "Do you accompany your friend?"

Klaus smiled—the mirthless expression Phil was beginning to know. "Roberto says I only have two tempi, slow and fast. But I play for him anyway." He paused, peering at Phil. "Unless you play."

"I'm very out of practice," he murmured, raising his drink to his lips as if it were a shield.

"You know what Yehudi Menuhin said." Klaus paused, peering at him. Phil shook his head. He had no idea what Yehudi Menuhin had said. Klaus continued triumphantly. " 'If I do not practice one day, I know it. If I do not practice two days, the critics know it. If I do not practice three days, the public knows it.' "

Phil frowned. It was an interesting point. He himself had discovered that he might stay away from the piano for several weeks and come back with new insight and authority. Something to do with the unconscious. He started to explain this but Klaus interrupted him.

"You cannot tell me practice is not necessary!" He was bobbing up and down with excitement. "Why did Rubinstein practice eight hours a day, even after fifty years?"

Phil started to reply that Rubinstein was famous for not practicing much but held his tongue. He had just realized that Klaus wasn't open to contradiction or even to intermediate shades of meaning. He was a binary person — on or off. If you were a pianist you practiced and that was that.

The feeling that he didn't belong here returned, more strongly than ever. He looked around the room again. He hadn't noticed a bronze sculpture in the corner. It looked like an Arp. Last month he hadn't been able to pay his rent without a loan from his brother. What was he doing in an apartment with a sculpture by Arp? Klaus was bending toward him now, his eyes huge and hungry. Phil shifted away. The thought of physical contact with his host was extremely unpleasant.

Just then the doorbell rang. "That is Roberto," Klaus announced, putting his drink on the coffee table without haste.

A slight dark man in his midthirties entered the room. Introductions were brisk and formal — Dr. Roberto Olivo, Mr. Philip Clark. But the newcomer wasn't one for formality. "Give me something to drink," he said, "and not that Campari shit." His voice was light and high, the vowels open — a Spanish tenor's voice, Phil thought.

"Klaus tells me you are a great pianist." He looked at Phil. His eyes were merry.

"He's never even heard me play."

"That's nothing. Klaus knows all about music." He raised his voice so that it carried to the kitchen. "You hear that, Lili? I said you know everything about music." He turned to Phil again. "I call him Lili Marlene. He really doesn't know anything about music. All he knows is how to make money."

Phil grinned. Maybe the evening wasn't going to be so bad after all. It turned out that Roberto was a specialist in the kidneys and genital tract. "At St. Luke's they call me the singing urologist," he laughed, "How do you like that?"

When Klaus returned with a scotch and soda, he said, "The roast will be ready in seventeen minutes. Perhaps we will have some music first."

"Give me four minutes with the scotch," Roberto said, winking at Phil, "and that will leave thirteen, just enough for *Dalla sua pace* if we take all the repeats."

Klaus brayed at that—the first time Phil had heard him laugh heartily. Then Roberto said, "Tell me how you're going to play tonight, Lili, fast or slow, I gotta make my adjustment."

It turned out that the singing urologist had a light voice, well-placed and true, but occasionally he pushed too hard. As for Klaus' accompaniment—it was steady, loud and uninspired. Most of the time he led rather than accompanied. As Phil sat listening, his fingers twitched slightly. He knew exactly how that piano line should go. Still, he applauded loudly when they finished.

"I think we got time for *Una furtiva lagrima*, what you say?" Roberto winked at Phil again. "But this time you gotta play fast or the dinner gets burned."

"No." Klaus stood up briskly. "I must do things in the kitchen. You will ask Phil."

They both turned toward him. Roberto was smiling but Klaus' blue gaze was flat and hard. And then, aware that he should not be nodding, not be getting up, not moving toward the piano, Phil heard himself say, "I really love that aria." In another moment he was on the padded stool, an expensive adjunct from Steinway, rotating the little wheels. Feeling dangerously suspended over a deep gulf, he tried a chord or two, then an arpeggio. The piano sounded quite different under his hands. The upper octaves were sweet and bell-like, the lower ones strong and mellow. He had never played on an instrument like this—not even for his graduation exam. It seemed molded to his inner ear, the outward expression of the tones he heard when he was alone. He had the brief impression that this piano had always been waiting for him and that he had only now, by chance or luck, intersected with it. And then, as he began the prelude to the aria he had the acute sensation that he was trapped beyond any hope of escape.

Roberto sang sweetly and gracefully in a lyric style that reminded Phil of Tagliavini. He was instantly aware that they teamed up well— bobbing together on the swells of the song, dipping into the troughs, holding back and pushing on with one impulse. When the last chord of the postlude faded away they both remained silent. For Phil, it was a familiar moment of repletion and exhaustion, one he had not experienced in a long time.

"You play very well." It was Klaus, standing in the kitchen door. Phil said nothing. He felt as if he had come home after a long absence. The room, so strange a few minutes ago, seemed to be slipping into familiarity.

He spread his hands over the keys, pressing them down soundlessly. Klaus and Roberto seemed to disappear. There were only the sounds waiting to be released. With a blind look upwards he began a trill— C#, D#—that merged into a cadenza spilling from his fingers like water. A moment later he was launched on the Debussy. The broken sevenths, the augmentations, slid off his fingers like translucent plates. In another moment he was in the midst of a surging vat of color, of green and silver splashes, darting opalescences and curtains of beaded light. And then, aware that he was plunging into the gulf he had hoped to avoid, he let himself hit bottom. A few minutes later he came out of the piece laughing and humming and thinking he should be wet from head to toe.

"*L'Isle Joyeuse*," Klaus announced, still in the kitchen door. "I have heard Gieseking play it."

Roberto was clapping. "He didn't play better than that."

Phil remained at the keyboard, not speaking, as their compliments arched over him. The music was decaying very slowly and he wanted to hear the last of it. The feeling of homecoming returned, more strongly. It was only when dinner was announced that he rose from the leather stool reluctantly. He really didn't want to leave the piano.

And then, as he moved toward the table, he had a sudden vision of his office, which was white and glarey, and where he sat all day looking into a dark screen which flashed numbers. A pain pierced his head. He hoped he wasn't going to get a migraine. And then, as quickly as it had appeared, his office vanished, and with it the pain.

He had been given the place of honor, facing the window with its view of Central Park and the blue-lit spires to the west. From this altitude the monoliths seemed rare and exotic, like crusaders' castles or the ziggurats of Nebuchadnezzar. Phil's sense of well-being expanded to include not only the marvelous vista but the table with its gleaming crystal, the lobster bisque in front of him, the superb wine poured into his glass. For one crazy instant he even imagined that all this was his. But a moment later he stopped himself. Why was he getting carried away? Money had produced all this—lots of it. He would never have that much.

He knew that making money was the sacred mission of every American, but he didn't have the gift. Maybe it was hereditary. His father had failed many times—as a vitamin salesman, a fertilizer distributor, a mail-order purveyor. Finally his mother had gone to work in a factory. The insecurity of those years, he knew, had left their mark. Perhaps they had contributed to his dislike for a performer's life.

"To our guest of honor," Klaus was holding up his wine glass, full of a golden Pouilly-Fuissé, "who will come back soon, I hope, and play again." Phil nodded and smiled. At the same time he wondered if he shouldn't nip all this in the bud. To mention again his decision to give up music. But somehow he couldn't. Besides, Roberto and Klaus had moved on to other topics. Roberto was now teasing Klaus. He turned to Phil.

"So this man, he comes here and looks at the piano and he says to Klaus, '*Ay, Diós*, what a nice big table.' "

Klaus laughed. "That man was a *jíbaro*," he informed Phil. "Do you know what that is?"

Phil shook his head. Klaus told him that a *jíbaro* was a Puerto Rican farmer. A rustic. "He had never seen a piano before, you can imagine what kind of primitive he was."

"With what you pay him, he could go out and buy one," Roberto observed.

Klaus grinned mirthlessly. "He did not get much, a few hundred dollars."

Phil found himself slightly embarrassed. If Klaus paid for sex that was fine, but he didn't really want to hear the details.

"I think Phil is shocked." Klaus was appraising him, his eyes a ferocious blue.

Phil protested but Klaus repeated his statement. He had the habit, Phil noticed, of repeating. Actually, he himself had on several occasions been offered money for sex. Many people found him attractive, drawn to his slender figure and ruddy skin, his eyes and hair of matching russet brown. But he had never accepted these offers.

"Yes, he is shocked," Klaus said for a third time. "He is a romantic."

Roberto waved his fork. "Maybe he has a lover."

"I do not think he does," Klaus replied.

Phil didn't like being discussed but he managed a smile. "Klaus is right. I don't." He saw no reason to discuss his love life. There had been affairs, female and male, but none had lasted more than a few months. He had always reached a point when he couldn't go on, when there seemed, well, nothing more to say.

Rosalind Karlinsky, a fellow student at Juilliard, had once observed to him—they were in her bed at the time, "You don't really need anybody, Phil, not deep down, that's your problem." Her eyes had gone dark with sarcasm and anger and he had been swept with guilt, but she had been right. Not that he hadn't tried to need her. God knows he'd done everything she'd asked and then some. But none of it had satisfied her and when she refused to see him any more he had felt mostly relief.

Klaus and Roberto were staring at him, waiting for details. His mind swept back again, this time to Justin Tolchin. He'd met Justin in a bar near Lincoln Center, a bar frequented by the music-ballet crowd, and they had embarked on an affair that very evening. Justin was a music-lover and this had sounded promising, but as the weeks wore on, Phil found Justin's endless talk about music more boring than anything else. It was as if Justin were speaking a secondhand language, made up of tired words and used phrases, because he couldn't find the primary one. Phil knew it was up to him to steer their relationship in a new direction, to give it passion and depth, but somehow he couldn't manage. At last, after a few months, by mutual consent, they stopped calling.

Klaus and Roberto had picked up their bantering, which continued throughout the meal. Phil insisted on clearing the table and loading the dishwasher. By the time he was through, the others were listening to some recordings of Panzera that Roberto had brought along. He left early—just after ten—pleading that he had to get up early for work. At the door, Klaus held his hand tightly in both of his and made him promise to return soon. Phil agreed. But on the way downtown his headache, which had held off all evening, returned.

He had a hard time getting to sleep that night. He went through most of his old repertoire in his mind, hearing it on the new piano, which made everything sound very fresh. Finally, exhausted after playing the Chopin B-minor Sonata, he fell asleep. Toward dawn he dreamed he was playing to a sold-out Carnegie Hall, with Rubinstein in the audience.

For the next few days, Phil found the office very difficult. The customers who called with complaints about their billing seemed angry or stupid. He had always liked talking to the foreigners who called—figuring out their meaning was a sonic game he enjoyed—but now he found himself irritated even by that. He had taken his job because it offered entry-level computer training with promise of more advanced training to come. But now, sitting in front of his little screen with its glare-proof mesh, he decided that the offer of promotion had been a lie. Some of the people in his department had been here for years without any further training. He was a rat in a maze of Hewlett-Packard terminals.

On the third night after his evening with Klaus he decided to make a thank-you call. He knew it wasn't really necessary. He also knew he wasn't eager to hear Klaus' meticulous English. At the same time he was aware that nothing could keep him from calling.

He was surprised to find that someone else answered—a younger, brighter American voice. When Phil asked for Klaus there was a hesitation. "Oh," came the reply, "you mean Ken." In another moment Klaus was on the line. His greeting was warm. He dismissed Phil's thank-yous and remarked, "You heard Buddy call me Ken, do not be surprised, it is a game we play."

Phil waited but more information was not forthcoming. He was about to hang up when Klaus said, "For the next three months I am away three days each week at one of our clients in Boston. If you wish to come here and play the piano, I give you the key. Tuesday and Wednesday night no one will bother you. I think you prefer that."

Phil was too surprised to answer. Worse, his heart had started a frenzied thumping, as if he had been threatened in some way. Klaus spoke again, explaining the ease, the privacy of the arrangement. Even the neighbors wouldn't mind. "You do not owe me anything," he concluded, "it is better for pianos to be used, *ja?*" He asked Phil to meet him at Lincoln Center on Saturday to pick up the key.

After hanging up, Phil sat by the phone for a long time. His forehead was cold and his palms were sweating. He should have said no. Nothing but trouble would come of all this. He didn't like piling up debts.

And then all these considerations were washed away in the opulence of the tones that rang in his ear. Two nights a week with the piano! Two nights a week with the instrument of his dreams! He could leave work and be at the apartment by five-thirty. That meant almost five hours of practice. He shuffled through his repertoire in his mind.

A recital program fell into place. It was just possible, just barely possible . . .

Klaus met him at the fountain in front of the opera house. He was going to hear a visiting troupe do *Rigoletto*. He had already spoken to his doorman; there would be no problem.

As Phil took the keys, he found himself full of something like self-loathing. He was being weak, indecisive. He had given up music and now he was slipping in again through the back door—a borrowed piano on borrowed premises. The first prizes in life, he knew, didn't go to people who changed their minds. Look at his father, forever abandoning one business to start another!

As he walked away from Klaus, aware for the last time of the intensity of his gaze, the unflickering blue of his eyes, the strict and mirthless line of his mouth, Phil thought he should turn around, return the keys and tell him to forget it. But even as he thought this he dismissed it. There was no way he could turn down the gift. The little metal objects in his hand would open the gates of paradise.

Phil found a note from Klaus waiting for him on the music-stand of the piano.

> Welcome to Phil. Food for your dinner is in the freezer, please help yourself. Be sure to turn off all lights before leaving. Thank you.
>
> Your friend,
>
> Klaus Ohmann

He had brought a sandwich in his satchel but he went to the kitchen to check. There was a selection of frozen gourmet meals, including boeuf bourgignon, manicotti, lemon sole and chicken Kiev. There was also a note about lighting the oven.

Feeling somewhat overwhelmed by all this kindness, he went back to the piano and began some runs. He had decided to spend the first hour each time on exercises. As he expected, his mind wandered while his fingers worked.

The last three days at work had taken a turn for the better. His boss had told him that a new class in programming was due to start on the first of the month. Phil would learn Cobol, the only one in Customer Complaints who was chosen. He'd get an hour off each day for class.

As if this weren't enough, his boss also said he'd be put in charge of several new employees fresh out of entry training. That meant another hour away from the monitor each day.

When Phil heard this, aware that he'd finally reached a turning point at the company, his first reaction was one of confusion. Things seemed to be piling up—first the Steinway and now this. He wondered if he'd be forced to some kind of major decision about it all.

When the hour of exercises was up he started work on the Beethoven Opus 101. It wasn't the hardest of the thirty-two sonatas or the easiest. About middling. He'd studied it before; now he wanted to see if anything had changed.

Around nine he stopped and heated the manicotti, which he ate standing up. It was quite good, all things considered. He only dirtied one fork, which he washed and replaced.

After dinner he began work on the Barber sonata. This, he had decided, would be the modern piece in his program. It was new and difficult.

It was only as he was leaving that he found the third and last note from his benefactor. It was taped to the inside of the front door. He hadn't noticed it when he came in.

> Goodnight, Phil. It was a pleasure to have you here, enjoying my piano.

Under that was the entire text (both stanzas) of the Schober poem, *An die Musik*, which Schubert had set. Phil stood by the door for some time, looking at Klaus' small, precise writing. Then, feeling rather spooked, he switched off the light.

That night he slept more peacefully than he had in months. Sleep enclosed him and kept him submerged for nine hours without a break. His first reaction, next morning, was to decide that practicing had exhausted him. But later he wasn't so sure. He thought it might instead have come from his new peace of mind. His life, both by day and night, now seemed full of satisfaction. He had the uneasy feeling that it was a satisfaction that only delayed, didn't answer, some important questions. Still, it was good to feel that his life was going somewhere.

His phone rang at eight o'clock that same morning. He knew right away who it was. The German voice was light and dry. "I am in Boston. You enjoyed your practice last night and also your dinner?" He replied that he had. "Good. Then you will continue and I will not bother you."

Phil was surprised. He was geared for a social request of some kind. But Klaus wanted him to be alone with the piano. To feel free. It seemed a little out of character, but before hanging up, Klaus let fall a remark that clarified this. "I am having a slight arterial problem," he said. "I must rest more in the evening and amuse myself less." He said goodbye promptly, so that Phil couldn't ask for details. But after hanging up, a wave of relief went through him. It seemed he had the piano with no immediate obligations. He was home free.

Over the next few weeks he didn't hear from Klaus directly. They communicated via little notes left in the apartment. His were mostly thank-yous, though he had bought several recordings and left them on the coffee table as gifts. Klaus' memoranda were mostly encouraging. He hoped Phil was making progress. He had had the piano tuned, did Phil notice? There was book on piano technique by Tobias Matthay in the bookcase near the window. Was the light adequate?

Although Klaus' notes were meant to be kind, Phil hated getting them. They made him feel the owner of the apartment was looking over his shoulder. That he was reminding Phil that all this didn't belong to him.

The fact was, he had come to regard the apartment as his own. This had been confirmed when he recalled an old saying of his mother's: "A house belongs to you if you sweep the floors and make the beds, whether the house is in your name or not." He didn't sweep floors or make beds but he had tended Klaus' apartment in other ways. He had filled it with music, spent his emotions there, his physical and intellectual strength—therefore it was his.

Sometimes, seated at the dining table with its wonderful view of the park—he had long since given up eating in the kitchen—he pretended that he really lived here. That the Barcelona chairs, the Bodhisattva and the Bokhara rug, even the sculpture by Arp, were items he had picked up at shops and galleries around town. It was a game, and sometimes he giggled at it, but still he found it oddly satisfying. What would his life have been like, he wondered, if he had decided to be a banker, like Klaus, or a doctor or lawyer? Would he now live in an aerie like this, high above the city, free of its turmoil and sweat and danger?

He always went back to the piano, after dinner, in an exultant mood. It seemed he had the best of both worlds.

As the weeks went by, Phil found his playing moving to a new plateau. Even though he only played two nights a week — a totally insufficient amount of time — he managed to reach levels closed to him before. Sometimes he had the impression he was turning into someone entirely different — no longer the mild, sweet-mannered Phil Clark who had played a few brilliant concerts then let the whole thing slip from his grasp, but a musician of formidable temperament, one of those tyrannical and theatrical personalities who electrify audiences. One night, on his way home, he thought of something his booking agent had told him. She had said she could predict a performer's entire career from the way he entered her office. She had made it clear, without actually saying so, that Phil hadn't entered her office in the right way. Well, all that was changing. He would enter that room — or any room — like a master now.

Of course, sometimes he had a few doubts, especially at bedtime. Then he would wonder if his new power and dedication were really so solid, if he were really turning into a titan of the keyboard. But most of the time these thoughts didn't occur to him.

One night, after playing a Chopin polonaise with a martial splendor that surprised him, he had lifted his eyes from the keyboard to see a castle, all shining turrets and walls, gleaming in E-major. It was a magic moment, giving him the temporary illusion that he was working not in tones but in stones, not in time but in space, and he had laughed out loud. Still, the mirage had stayed with him for a long time. It seemed to symbolize his new life.

And things at work had improved too. The course in Cobol turned out to be interesting and easy. He'd always been good at math, had always loved the way numbers combined and separated, and now he found solving problems in computer language a pleasure. Algorithms seemed the culmination of logic and order — sometimes he wished all of life could be broken into component parts so neatly. At other times, though, he thought it odd that he should respond both to numbers and to music. They seemed to represent opposing spheres of human thought. Why should he find it challenging to write a program that would read in integers X representing the change in cents to be given to a customer in a minimal number of coins . . . and that very evening build a glowing edifice out of a Beethoven sonata? What connection could there be between the two? Was there something he had overlooked — some final link — that had not yet been revealed to him?

Toward the end of the third month, Klaus called him on the week-end. His voice sounded strange to Phil, an echo from some forgotten world of obligation. He had to remind himself not to be curt, not to treat Klaus like a caller at Customer Complaints. But he needn't have worried. Klaus spoke less assuredly, less emphatically. He didn't even repeat any of his statements. He seemed to have gotten a little fuzzy around the edges. Several times he had to stop for breath. Only once did he refer to his condition, saying, "My arterial trouble has gotten a little worse." Phil didn't ask any questions—it seemed to be a subject full of hidden traps—and the upshot of the call was that Phil was to come to the apartment, play his program for Klaus and give back the keys.

Strangely, this ultimatum didn't upset Phil. It didn't really seem the end of anything. He was positive that his connection with the Steinway was not about to be terminated.

He worked very hard on his program for the remaining two prac-tice sessions—polishing, refining, searching out new details. It seemed that his life was coming to some kind of climax, though he couldn't say exactly why.

Klaus met him at the door. Phil was shocked by the change in his appearance. His roundness was gone. His skin seemed draped over vanished flesh. He was paler and had stopped dyeing his hair. It was almost completely white.

"You find me changed." It was a statement, not a question. Phil murmured politely but Klaus interrupted. "I have been on a special diet, plus new medication. I have lost twenty-five pounds."

He ushered Phil inside, touching his arms and back several times, but without the urgency of former times. Looking around the room with its familiar furnishings, Phil felt briefly disoriented. With Klaus in residence everything seemed different, as if the chairs and tables had tilted or shifted. But the Steinway hadn't changed. It was still as sleek and beautiful as ever.

Klaus wanted to hear the news. Phil talked about his practicing, about his belief that he had broken through to a new level of pianism, that his job was going well, and that he had been wondering if his future lay with music or with computers.

Klaus listened, his mouth set in a straight line, his eyes less ferocious than formerly. From time to time he nodded. When Phil finished he sat silently. Then, surprisingly, he changed the subject.

"I enter the cardiology unit at New York-Cornell in two weeks. I am going to have bypass surgery."

His voice was matter-of-fact but Phil heard a plea behind it. "I'm sure the operation will be a big success," he replied quickly. "I keep reading about them . . . they seem to be a dime a dozen these days."

"I hope so." Klaus' voice was faint. He pressed his fingertips to his chest. "I do not want to die." He stared at Phil, his eyes timid behind the gold frames. Then he said, "I want to make up for a rather selfish life. I have decided to make a new will."

Phil was aware that his heart had started drumming, a signal of fear. But what was he afraid of?

"Yes, a new will. The old one left everything to my sister who is in Frankfurt, but that is silly. Her husband left her all what she needs. I have decided to leave my friend Buddy money for his acting school and I have decided to leave the Steinway to you. I do not know you well but I like you. Do you want it?"

Phil stood up and went to the window. He had to catch his breath. The drumming in his chest had speeded up. He also felt slightly dizzy, as if a terrible decision had to be made.

"You do not answer me. Do you want it?"

There. He was in control of his breathing, his balance. He turned from the pale spires of the skyscrapers across the park to find Klaus peering at him. A faint, mirthless smile played on his lips.

"I think the operation will be a complete success, Klaus. But if you want to leave me the Steinway, which I'm sure will never happen, that would be okay."

There, he'd said it. Said it with control and a measure of dignity. Klaus was still peering at him. His eyes were blank, his slight smile unreadable. At last he said, "Good. I think we have an understanding. And now, perhaps, you will play."

Phil moved toward the piano slowly, as if on wheels. The music waiting there seemed the only certitude in a sea of mixed emotions. In another moment he would be cleansed, purified. He would speak the only language that made perfect sense.

He sat down, rotating the little wheels on the stool quite unnecessarily. Then he dropped his hands and began the F-major Prelude from the second Book. By the time he got to the Fugue he had forgotten all the confusion of the last few minutes.

The night before the operation Phil went to see Klaus in the hospital. He found him calm on the surface but angry and apprehensive underneath. Klaus found fault with everything—the room, the nurses, the food. Phil had the impression that Klaus thought he had been cheated of something, but whether it was of desirable accommodations or of life itself he wasn't sure.

At any rate, listening to the trivial complaints, Phil found himself unable to reply. He seemed to have lost control of things. As Klaus showed him how his body hair had been shaved off, Phil thought that he had ceded his future to Klaus and to his surgeons. Then he recalled his feelings when he had first accepted the keys to the apartment. He had seen, quite clearly, that the first prizes didn't go to the people who were indecisive. But here he was, waiting for chance or fate or Klaus' heartbeat to decide his future.

Because, in the last two weeks, he had decided that if he inherited the piano he would quit his job and devote his life to music. This had come to him in the evenings at home when he had been deprived of the Steinway, when his life had been reduced to echoes and memories. He knew it was wrong to let everything ride on an inheritance. If he were really determined to revive his music, there were ways to get a piano just as good—maybe with a bank loan. But even as he realized this, he knew he wouldn't act on it. There was something else in the equation, something he hadn't figured out yet, but Klaus' piano was part of it.

He kissed Klaus goodbye—a brush of his lips on his forehead. The skin was icy. Phil wondered if he was being hypocritical in wishing him good luck tomorrow morning, then banished the thought. He did wish him good luck. He didn't want him to die on the operating table. His final awareness, as he went down in the elevator, was that you could probably never write an algorithm that would encompass all the variables of this situation.

He called the hospital several times the following day but was only told Mr. Ohmann was still in the O.R. At last, unable to stand the suspense, he left work and went there. He found Roberto Olivo in the waiting area of the cardiac floor. Roberto had just seen Klaus as he was wheeled from the operating room. Klaus had been covered with dried blood, waxy and pale, but had managed to squeeze Roberto's hand. "He's gonna be okay," Roberto remarked in an offhand way. "I got the feeling Lili is too mean to die."

Phil had laughed, wondering if Roberto knew about the new will, hoping he didn't. It would make his own presence here somewhat ambiguous. At last the surgeon who had headed the surgical team came into the area. He was an East Indian, Dr. Govokind. "I took out all five," he observed casually, with a wave of his hand. "As long as we were in there, why not?" Roberto let out a low whistle. "Quintuple bypass," he whispered. "He is doing fine," Dr. Govokind added, quite breezily, "you can go in now, he is all cleaned up. No more than two minutes, please."

Phil followed Roberto into the room. Klaus was lying on his back, his eyes open. He looked very small and vulnerable. "How are you?" Phil murmured, feeling foolish. Klaus didn't reply. A slight smile played on his lips and Phil wondered if the smile wasn't simply an automatic contraction of the mouth muscles.

"I told Phil you're too mean to die." Roberto leaned over the bed, looking directly into Klaus' eyes. They focused for a moment, then the lips moved. "*Ja. Ja.*" Then Klaus closed his eyes and they left.

Phil went to the hospital three times. On the second day after the operation, when Klaus was still pale but able to speak; five days later, when his rosy color had returned; and on the day he was able to walk, when his room was full of flowers, fruit, books. On this visit, Klaus bared his scar—an angry welt that ran from throat to navel.

Phil registered Klaus' progress with something like relief. The decision had been made; the future had been taken out of his hands. At the same time he wondered if he would really be able to spend the rest of his life doing sterile acrobatics inside an artificial brain.

The thought depressed him and he found himself, during the weeks of Klaus' recovery, lapsing into melancholy. He knew the depression was caused by something hidden, something unacknowledged, but when he went to search for it, he couldn't find it. It seemed to shine, or glimmer, just beyond his reach, rather like the mirage of the castle in E-major. During this period he was also losing his finger dexterity, gained over the last few months at the price of so many boring arpeggios. This didn't help his mood either.

Finally the day of Klaus' discharge was scheduled. Phil offered to take him home, but Klaus said he would prefer to see Phil a month or two after that. "When I am strong again," he said, peering through the gold-rimmed spectacles which had now been reinstated, along with the gold hair and the gold wristwatch. His eyes, when he said this, were of the ferocious blue that Phil remembered. When Phil bent over the bed to plant a goodbye kiss on Klaus' forehead, Klaus reached out and squeezed his shoulder in a grip as fierce and possessive as he had used on their first evening together. Phil had to break away.

Almost two months went by before Klaus phoned Phil to ask him to visit. During that time Phil had forced himself not to think about music. His depression had lifted, to be replaced by a general bleakness. He wondered if he would feel bleak for the rest of his life.

When he arrived at the apartment, he found Klaus at the door dressed in a blue robe from Sulka. It appeared he had nothing on underneath. The scar, visible in the opening of the robe, had paled to a thin line. He greeted Phil cheerfully. "It is good to see you under more pleasant circumstances." He took Phil's hands in his. "I prefer entertaining my friends in my own home."

Phil found all this warmth unsettling. Moving past Klaus, he walked to the middle of the living room. It had reverted to its original strangeness. It seemed odd, inexplicable, that he had ever felt it was his. Evidences of Klaus' convalescence were everywhere — in a spread of get-well cards on the piano, in a huge new ficus by the window, in a treadmill installed in a corner. It was no longer a shrine to music, Phil thought, but merely an outer skin for a wealthy man. Even the piano seemed smaller, less imposing, as if it too had shrunk in importance compared to Klaus.

Klaus was staring at him. Phil wondered if he should tell him about all his conflicts of the past few weeks, about his plans and hopes and depression. Did their friendship — and they had probably shared enough to qualify as friends — require that kind of honesty? And then he forgot all that in the shock of Klaus' next remark.

"You thought I would die," said the little man, whose plumpness, Phil could see, was now returning. "Yes." He spoke quite matter-of-factly. "You hoped I would die. Please do not be embarrassed. Bankers understand human nature."

Phil stood in the center of the room. He was unable to speak. A freezing shame poured through him.

"If I had died, this would have been yours." Klaus tapped the case of the piano, which now looked to Phil like a black coffin. "It is worth twenty-five thousand dollars."

Klaus' glasses glittered under the track lighting. Then he moved close to Phil, so that his slightly swollen belly pressed into Phil's side.

The muscles of his mouth pulled back into what appeared to be a smile but which Phil knew now was only a rictus of desire. "I want you to make this apartment your own. To come here and play any time."

Phil started to move away, but Klaus' hand was on his arm, detaining him. "You will come any time but now we will go inside, *ja?*" He jutted his chin in the direction of the bedroom.

"No." He had found his voice at last. "I really don't want to."

Klaus was pushing into his side, his lips curled. Phil felt the stirrings of desire there, even as his own flesh chilled. "Perhaps you would like first some refreshment?"

With a jerk he freed himself. "What is the matter, Phil?" Klaus was peering at him as if he were behaving irresponsibly.

"I'm leaving."

"You cannot leave, Phil. Not yet." The blue eyes widened.

And then, as Klaus approached again and Phil knew he would have to fend him off physically, he understood why he had built a dream career around this apartment, this piano. He was a person who required extra amounts of safety. It was a result of his father's endless failing and his mother's endless sorrow. But safety was a commodity that had to be paid for like any other. Like bread or gas or potatoes. And now the bill was coming due.

"*Komm, komm.*" Klaus was touching him again, his voice harsh. He was, Phil understood, no longer inviting but commanding.

And then, as he shook his head, a final realization rushed toward him. His music only came to him when he felt safe. It was not just Klaus' piano that he wanted, but everything that went with it—the apartment and the furnishings and the food in the freezer and, yes, even the view. He wanted, in effect, another life. "I'm sorry, Klaus, I really am."

He was moving toward the door now, aware that Klaus was turning burgundy with rage. He hoped his new veins wouldn't be affected. He opened the door, then stepped into the hall. Behind him he heard gutturals of outrage and breaking glassware. "I'm sorry," he murmured again, closing the door. As he walked to the elevator he knew he had seen the last of this particular apartment. And then, for the third and last time, he said, "I'm sorry." And he was, truly. Because he just glimpsed his future and it was filled with numbers—a wilderness of numbers stretching as far as the eye could see.

Backwards

The beginnings are always the hardest. Learning how to walk when your legs are weak, how to run when your breath comes short, how to go to the bathroom without soiling your clothes. Of course, there are people here at the Happy Village to help you. I don't always remember their names, so I make up my own. The Purple Blimp, who wheezes when she pushes my wheelchair up the ramp. The Angel, a young man who gives me my bath every morning and whose cheeks are as firm and round as nectarines. The Illustrated Man, whose tattoos change color according to the time of day. Mighty Mouse. The Piston.

Of course, the boredom is the worst part. Nothing happens. Sometimes I wheel myself out to the veranda to watch the sailboats on the Bay. I try to imagine what it might be like to sit in the scuppers, one hand on the tiller, the canvas beating overhead, the gulls crying. Yes, what will it be like when I'm younger—forty, thirty, twenty? It will be a world of excitement I can hardly imagine now.

Last week Bradley brought me the recorder into which I'm dictating these remarks. He delivered it in his usual flat, hostile way. "Here, Morley, you can yap into the microphone and you won't have to drive everybody crazy." He deposited it on my lap, making his usual joke about Morley the Trombone. My last name is Trumbull and it's a joke I don't much appreciate. I scowl but he sits on the foot of my bed and pretends not to notice. Still, I can see the familiar expresion on his face. Kind of tight and squinched up, as if he'd just swallowed a turd. I call it Bradley's Hating Look. Yes, hate is the dominant emotion between us, though I like to think it's more on his side than mine. And why shouldn't we hate each other? Two old men who know too much. Who know all the necessary truths, in fact. Trust no one. Resist de-

dependency. Love is a fiction. Violence lurks everywhere.

And yet we go on—don't ask me why. Bradley returns each day—he's very spry, heredity, I guess—and sits on my bed. He tries, unsuccessfully, to disguise his squinched-up look and we discuss the future. Where we will live when I am discharged from the Happy Village. What kind of careers we are to have. How to manage the changes that lie ahead of us.

I have a vague idea of what I want to do, but I don't mention it to Bradley. Only trouble will come of that. It's something I have to hold inside, allow to unfold in solitude. He's too full of hate to let me have it happily.

It has to do with the theater. Yes, the stage. I have felt faint stirrings at night, when I lie in my bed and listen to the snores of my roommate, old Harbison. I want to make something beautiful of my life. I want to make it an emblem of a better world. And one night I had a vision that convinced me my choice was right. I saw myself in tights, magenta tights that showed off my handsome legs. (No director would ever have to put me in boots!) As I paced the stage, handsome as a god, embracing a whole series of heroines—Juliet, Mary Stuart, Saint Joan, Millamant—the audience roared with admiration and delight. Morley Trumbull, the handsomest pair of legs in show business!

How Bradley would scoff if he knew. ("It might help if you could act instead of showing off your calves.") But of course, his real emotion would be jealousy. Watching him as he sits on the foot of my bed, talking about companionship, I know that his deepest fear is that I might succeed where he fails. He needs my ailments, my inadequacies. They make him feel strong.

And yet, we go on. We both know there is no alternative. It will be Bradley and Morley for the foreseeable future, as if each of us were softened, molded, to receive the imprint of the other. And—to be honest—I need his weaknesses too. His impracticality, his impulsiveness, his ready anger. I want to be cool for both of us. And so we interlock at all levels, good and bad.

My discharge has come through! I am to leave next Tuesday. Bradley helped engineer it—he has found us a little house in Pacific Acres—and the authorities believe I can manage. For the first time since my arrival, this place seems attractive, almost appealing. I can wake up, eat, walk, use the potty, sleep—all without the slightest effort. Everything is done for me. Why must I try for more? What is the urge that makes me light out for the greater world?

The night before my departure I have a terrible dream, more hurtful than any I can remember. It was quite simple—merely a conversation with the grass. But it comes back to me, insisting, as I pack in the morning. "Listen," the tiny green spears whisper as they wave in a long sweep, "listen." And then a sigh runs along that emerald harp and they cry, "Every centimeter of new green costs us an agony beyond measure." The message shudders along my spine as I snap my bag: *The grass does not want to grow.*

By the time Bradley and I reach our new home, that message is forgotten, thank goodness. More important things come up—how we are to furnish this little house of weathered shakes, what rooms we will choose for this and that, who our neighbors are.

He has begun to question me about my plans too. Several times I almost let it out—my secret dream of a career onstage. But each time I catch myself. It will come out in time but I want to be sure, first. I don't want Bradley destroying it from the very beginning.

I've chosen an attic room for myself. Bradley sleeps on the second floor. There's a skylight right over my bed, so I can see the clouds wandering—wisps of gauze that change color every hour. I love to lie flat and stare at them as they cross my little square of glass. I prefer that to reading or listening to the radio. Bradley, by the way, is a fierce reader. He buys several books every day—books on the most diverse, arcane subjects. I don't believe he'll get around to reading all of them for years.

We're a little awkward with each other. There seems to be so much to protect against—as if behind our sharp bones and scored flesh, contoured like relief maps, there were other, sharper dangers. We know too much. We were born that way. But sometimes, when the clouds above me are particularly soft, when I imagine I am in a glass-bottomed boat turned upside down on the sea of the sky, I wonder if we really know too much or if we merely know the wrong things.

Sometimes at night I can hear Bradley turn over in his bed just below me. His groans strike me as the saddest human sound there is—the charges leveled by the flesh against gravity or God. One night, after hearing him groan, I got up and went downstairs to look at him. Even though I tiptoed, the stairs gave off little squeaks of alarm, like an emperor's canaries. Something was pulling me down—something

I hadn't felt in the six months I'd been in the house. I stood over his bed for a long time. I saw a grim little man, peeled down to bone, his hands balled into angry fists by his head. But even as I stood there, something trembled in me. I felt—what? Not desire, exactly, but the hint of it. A brief image of how that skin will smooth out, the muscles expand, the endoskeleton flex into postures of grace. Another night, during my secret visit, he woke up. Perhaps he heard the stirring, the trembling, in me. "Are you spying on me, Morley?" he hissed, sitting up suddenly, eyes aflame. I left, murmuring apologies. I was guilty, confused. What did I really have in mind? Suddenly it seemed better to stay in my attic bedroom, not to explore our future, not to change. *The grass does not want to grow.*

Bradley has slipped and broken a small bone in his ankle. He is immobilized in a cast for six weeks. This happened early in the second year of our life together. I had made my first attempt at a career— acting class with an excellent teacher downtown—and had to tell Bradley. He seemed to take it well, perhaps because he was launched on his own training as a librarian. It seemed both of us had found pursuits that satisfied us. But his fall, his broken bone, changed the status quo somewhat. We had remained as before—I in my attic scanning the sky, Bradley holed up in bed, staving off the world with tight fists and angry groans—but now I had to bestir myself. Carry food, help him to the bathroom, find him new books and magazines.

One day, bringing him a washcloth, I suggest I wash his back for him. Our eyes meet—his a delicate hazel, the color of aspens in fall—and I feel a slight gap in the hatred between us. A hint that better times, better feelings, might lie ahead. It seemed that we might expand our list of necessary truths—not yet, but soon. It was only an instant, and we didn't talk about it, but as I washed his back (skin so white, tendons so long and fine), I thought that we did not have to keep faith with what we had learned so far.

But after drying him off, sensing his withdrawal—almost a physical shrinking of his skin under my fingertips—I put away the thought. Men hate more steadily than they love, I reminded myself. Why should Bradley and I be any different? Besides, hatred is as strong a bond as love. I shouldn't complain, after all. Don't we have each other's company? Don't we have this little nest under the visiting clouds? What more can I expect?

My career has taken a turn for the better. John Hauser, director of the Neighborhood Thespis League, has offered me a nice part in an upcoming production. No magenta tights, alas, but a very nice scene with a dragon sister-in law. John heard, or saw, something in my audition (I did a soliloquy from Richard II) that excited him enough to cast me. His instincts are very sound because *Another Language* couldn't be more different from Shakespeare. Absolutely plain, no fancy language, no breast-beating or melodramatics.

I give a lot of thought to breaking the news to Bradley. At last, after an especially delicious breakfast of sausage and French toast (his favorite), I let it drop casually. "John is thinking of casting me in *Another Language*." Not much reaction—an encouraging sign—and I continue. "A small part, not too taxing." A hypocritical sigh follows. "I guess I'll find out whether I have it or not."

I know perfectly well that I have it in spades, but I'm not about to announce it to Bradley. My speech floats around the sunlit kitchen and lands on the sugar bowl like a fly. He nods and continues reading the newspaper. A little gust of relief goes through me, compounded with disgust. Why do we circle each other like this, stepping around our pettiness and egotism? Why don't we take pride and pleasure in each other's efforts?

A useless thought. I choke it off by getting up and washing the dishes.

Bradley came to the opening. I willed him out of my mind, blocking the thought that he was in the audience, as I went into my big scene with the monstrous sister-in-law and was rewarded with the best hand of the evening. If I had thought about Bradley I'd never have been able to get out a word. Of course, I am instantly at the height of my powers.

He came to the green room afterwards. "You were good, Morley," he said in his flattest, most uninflected voice. I looked at him. We had both changed in the years we had been living together but his alterations were suddenly very visible. His head was straighter, prouder, on the column of his neck, his chest was fuller and thicker, his hands were free of the speckles of age. Middle age was settling on him with a massive grace. But did he mean it when he said I was good? I peer into his eyes. No information there. A wave of guilt sweeps over me—quite unwarranted, I know. Has my success diminished Bradley? Have I failed him in some way? He seems to be scrutinizing me angrily. Will I ever know what goes on behind those stern features, those eyes the color of fallen aspen leaves?

Two nights later I'm awakened suddenly. The moon is down. Bradley is standing over me. My first reaction is pleasure, but when I hear his voice I freeze. "Damn you, Morley, damn you." He seems to be speaking automatically, from some blind, dead part of himself. I whisper something reassuring, try to plead with him — as if I'd done something wrong! — but my words are puny against the wall of his anger. And then I see the gun, blue-black in the haze of the descended moon. "Bradley!" I scramble back, clutching the blankets as if they were armor. But it isn't physical fear that destroys me. No, it's the realization that we are both weapons pointed at each other, living affronts, avengers. I hear a click. The safety is released. A vast passivity seizes me. So this is the way it ends.

The next minute there's a strangled sob and the sound of steel clattering. I see his form bending under the eaves as he moves off. He goes downstairs quickly. A moment later I retrieve the gun. It is heavy with hatred.

The next morning Bradley comes down with a raging fever. The doctor can't help, nor penicillin or mycin. He is in the grip of some vast, incoherent malady. For two weeks he lies on the couch in the living room. At last, pale and thin, he rallies.

Bradley's brain fever — that's what it was — seems to have cleared the air. No mention of his visit to the attic. I've dropped the gun in the Bay. And then, to my surprise, a month after recovering, he urges me to audition for another part, a bigger one. "You can do it, Morley, you're better than any of them." I can hardly believe my ears. Or my eyes. Because Bradley is looking at me with something like humor. He puts out his hand and rubs my arm. Not long, not hard, but enough so that a new necessary truth pops into my head: the true lover says yes. An absurd notion, but it comes again in expanded form: the true lover says yes over the noisiness of your own no.

Is our solitude, our shared loneliness, about to end? Is our hatred exhausted — a hatred bred in brittle bones and scored skins and disillusion like a grey sheet drawn over the face of the world? My arm still tingles where he rubbed me.

Bradley stands up suddenly, as if he too were perturbed by this new possibility. He says he's going out for a walk. I sit silently, my hand on my arm. I feel lost amid a sea of books. Our living room is awash in volumes, the detritus of Bradley's endless curiosity. And then, picking up one of them, I realize what has fed my attraction to Bradley. It is that he knows things. Knows why the sea is salt, what keeps an airplane up and why computers remember things. Knows the names of the stars and the roadside weeds and how all that naming started. The power, the sexiness of knowledge! The realization bursts through the surface of my mind and I am aware of a new lustfulness. Not the placid desire, tinged with melancholy, which has filled me until now but something fiercer, more dangerous. I imagine Bradley's body as it might look under my sky-window, crossed by shadows of clouds. The world, our customary world, seems to recede slightly. New bodies, new hopes.

But old habits don't die easily. After my next show, in which I get to wear tights, though of a somber black, I find Bradley's sullenness has returned. Maybe we are moving too fast. Several nights I sneak down to his room and stand over him, only to find him watching me through slitted eyes. What do we want? What do we expect? A midnight visit to his bed no longer brings an accusation of spying, thank heavens, but there is still fear.

And then one night, climbing back to my attic, I realize that we prefer the ill will, the discomfort, to newer and stranger feelings. To explore is to cast off, to be swept away. Who wouldn't cling to shore? And so Bradley's sullenness seems a signal of home, and I stop my midnight visits.

But our evenings have taken on new excitement. Bradley talks to me of scientific marvels and the wonders of the ancient world and the habits of birds. I forget where I am, in the delight of that learned recital. And then, after a few months, my seducible heart starts to buzz again and I feel my veins sizzle and bulge. Once again I know there is no escape—not for Bradley, not for me. We are imprinted on each other, each visage the one behind the many. Bradley has told me about Plato and I think that clever Greek might have been right about the Ideal, though I can never think about it too long or I get muddled. I never had a head for abstractions. Detail is what I love—the whorl of a petal, the brush of an eyelash, the gleam of a saucer. If I stare into space too long my head fills up with the emptiness of great ideas. Still, as Bradley expounds Plato and I watch his face, fuller now, burgeoning with a hint of youthfulness, it seems that there is a grand design, a single plan, and that Plato knew it before anyone else.

And then one night it happens. After a cast party for an Ibsen play.

We'd been drinking but that wasn't the real reason. In point of fact, we were ready.

We got home after midnight, but instead of separating as usual we moved to the kitchen. I had just suggested a cup of tea when Bradley moved toward me. Suddenly he was hunkered down in front, his arms around my waist, his head on my lap. I touched his hair—no longer grey and crinkled but a soft chestnut glinting here and there with gold.

And then it came to me how little we had said over the years. Silence had enclosed us, broken now and then by some trivial remark. Nothing important seemed worth the bother of putting into words. What difference would they make? How could they possibly bridge the gap between us? But now, with Bradley's lustrous mop under my fingertips, I am possessed by the desire to talk, to tell him everything. How I love his nighttime lectures, how I am terrified of a certain emptiness, how the mystery of the world can be parsed, explained, solved. Why did I ever believe such sentences were useless?

And so I start to say the things I'd never bothered with before. Bradley raises his head and looks at me. He is, I know, seeing me anew. Seeing past my smooth skin and clear face into an interior which he did not know existed. His hazel eyes lose their focus. He is forgetful of self as he listens and I know we have passed some old barrier for good.

At last he puts his mouth to mine. His tongue is fierce against my lips. We pull back, breathing hard. "Let's go inside, Morley." He motions toward his bedroom, where I have passed so many midnights trying to read our future in the twists of his torso, his balled fists, his groans.

A moment later we're peeling off our clothes, blood pounding, eyes starting with new sights (when had he sprouted all that chest hair?) and a new necessary truth pops into my head: trust somebody. As we tumble onto the bed I say it out loud: trust somebody. He doesn't hear me and it doesn't matter.

We're new at this but there's a natural order that asserts itself. Why did God give us parts if not to use them? As we experiment, we go off into giggles. Who would have thought we could discover so many wonderful fits? Bodies are full of interlocking parts. At last the giggles subside and we help each other to the high plateau where, I am suddenly convinced, we will spend the rest of our lives.

As we settle down for sleep, neither wanting to leave the other for the night, I marvel at the fact that this happened only after so much waiting. Why had I believed in the end of things before I saw their beginning? Why had I thought we would be strangers forever when I had only to reach out and touch? Feeling Bradley's body nestled into mine I can only wonder at the partial vision which obscures each stage of life, at the truths which appear to be necessary but may only be convenient.

And so a new existence begins. Bradley has forgiven me—or decided to overlook—my professional success. At the same time he is having great success of his own. Some of his free lectures at the library—given to growing crowds of admirers—have attracted the attention of publishers. He is invited to write some books. An encyclopedia board offers him a chair. A TV crew comes to town; he will appear on a game show called Information Bowl.

The years seem to be perfectly balanced, at work and at home. Bradley has his elite, adoring public; I have good parts in important productions. In the season when I triumph triply as Macbeth, Trigorin and Ernest, he is invited to the White House for dinner.

Our happiness abroad overflows at home. We sleep together in the attic now, under the sky-window, where we scrutinize each other for hours, by lamplight and moonlight, noting details which give new pleasure: the hollow of a throat, the little valley where the thigh locks into the trunk, the drifting eddies of hair. There is nothing we cannot do together, no fear which cannot be shared, no joy which cannot be celebrated. The swirl of our blood matches the swirl of the world. We are often invited into homes just so people can observe us together.

And then, little by little, the excitement of my career begins to pall. Maybe the enthusiasm of starting out is gone. But one night I have a clear vision of a future filled with boredom. Why am I dressing up in other people's words and lives? Why do I need all this acclaim?

When I tell Bradley this he nods quickly, the tossing shake that signifies he has been thinking about the same thing. "Sometimes I think if I have to answer one more question . . ." he doesn't finish, just sits glumly. He is slimmer now, lighter. It occurs to me that we are mutating from hard-working grubs to butterflies, from husk to flower. Perhaps our job is merely to bloom.

One night, soon afterward, he tells me that the brain secretes a substance that makes us forget. This fluid, whose name I can't recall, saves us from the past, wipes the slate clean, so that we can only look ahead, plan, hope. When he says this I cast my mind back, trying to remember. What did I call that heavy black woman at the Happy Village who pushed me up ramps in my wheelchair? What did I speak into my tape recorder? What was Bradley's nickname for me? Everything has faded. Another memory nudges at me, something about a gun. Did Bradley really hate me to the point of murder once?

I don't know who suggested the trip to Europe, but we both knew that the time had come for our honeymoon. A long trip—we plan to stay away at least a year—means the end of our careers, but neither of us cares. We haven't really cared for several years. We have both begun to forget our skills, preferring to spend time dreaming or walking or running, our heads as empty as the sky. I have no idea now how to hold an audience, how to charm the people who give out the parts, how to walk quietly into a room and hold every eye. And Bradley doesn't seem to be sure of his facts any more. Last week he got two of the pharaonic dynasties confused. He didn't even care. A few years ago he would have sat up all night rememorizing the list, from Hatshepsut to Ptolemy.

And so the day of our departure arrives. It's going to be a grand tour, a dazzling procession of palaces, ports, galleries. A journey of wonder and discovery, the climax of everything.

It is in Paris that we have our last and greatest quarrel, proof (as if we needed it) that we live more intensely in each other's company than any place else on earth.

It started in a restaurant, Le Chien Qui Fume, where a new friend, name of Chester Maynard, had joined us for dinner. Chester was staying at our hotel, a fleabag near the Sorbonne (we had reached the age of youthfulness and insolvency). He was a southern boy, with a poorly-defined chin, squinty eyes, airbrushed hair. I thought of him as a walking pudding.

At one point during dinner, Chester made a pass at me. It wasn't unusual, of course—I had grown into a handsome young man—but for some reason Bradley took it very amiss. After Chester had drawled out his double entendre and squeezed my knee, Bradley picked up the carafe of wine and poured it down the front of his shirt. Chairs were overturned, waiters aroused, punches exchanged. We were made to pay for a meal we hadn't eaten, ushered to the door and told never to return.

Bradley, striding beside me through the leafy streets, refuses to speak, but I don't mind. In fact, I am full of a throttling joy. Bradley is jealous! I recall, with an effort, his earlier envies. This is very different. In the old days he'd been acting from an empty heart; this time his heart is full.

When we get back to the hotel we have a shouting match. The usual accusations—we have read about them in cheap novels, but now we let fly with a melodrama that is new to us. It seems that strangers are screaming at each other. A few minutes later we're on the floor, tearing, hurting, punishing. But it's a warm anger, a fury hiding love, and the inevitable happens. Before long we're grappling with passion on that filthy carpet, our supple bodies reflected in the giant *armoire à glace* alongside. Even as I maltreat Bradley's slender body, I adore it. Only once, near the end, am I aware of a paradox: how the body invites and then prevents true union. By the time we finish, the awareness is gone.

Bradley remains on his back. Loss and death are all around—in the grimy mirror, the tattered chairs, the wet spots on the dirty rug. We have plated the room with gold for a few minutes but now it's uglier than ever. Bradley's forearm is over his eyes and it takes me a few minutes to realize he is weeping.

"What's wrong?" He doesn't answer. His chest heaves. "Don't cry, Brad."

And then I know he's right to cry. Why not, after all? I roll over on my stomach, wondering if it hadn't been better when we were old and full of mistrust. Those were minor pains compared to these.

"Don't you see?" He sits up, his nose red, his eyes bloodshot. "Don't you see?"

I try to reassure him but without conviction. Our mutual need, our hopeless dependency, lies on us like a deformity. We are both cripples at heart. I see it as clearly as he does.

At last, exhausted, we burrow into the bed and sleep. When I wake up, I discover that a new necessary truth has blown into my ears: the whole world is my home. The notion took up residence while I slept, the shining residue of our struggle on the floor.

It's hard breaking the news to Bradley. In fact, I wait until we get back to tell him he's been replaced by something larger, more general. He feels betrayed, of course—at first, anyway. It's only later, when his own changes come, that he accepts it.

I begin to look at children more closely, at the fierceness with which they feed on life, at their greed in eating, sleeping, speaking. Sometimes, watching an infant grasp a toy, I am struck by the simplicity of it all. One day I shall be as old as a baby.

Of course, there are times when I resist change, remembering my dream in the nursing home, clinging to Brad and the old comfortable love. But these resistances become fewer. Not long after returning from Europe I insist that he move downstairs, out of the attic room. I don't want to be interrupted in my progress. He doesn't mind. He too is exhausted by our years together. He wants out of that slavery as much as I.

As the years go by I see him less and less. Most of the time I'm outside, playing in the street with new friends. Sometimes, in the middle of scrimmage, or a game of hide-and-seek, I reflect on the long voyage now coming to an end. Its purpose, I see now, was only to bring me here, to this field, waiting to be tagged or raced or wrestled. It was for this I mastered all the changes of mind and spirit and gland. A shudder ripples through me as this discovery expands. I have passed through solitude and doubleness in order to merge into every particle around me — the trees, the dirt, the bricks of the school, the dresses of the girls, the flashing faces and quicksilver forms of my teammates. I am at the peak of existence, closer to birth than ever before.

And then, as more time goes by and I move forward into the rapid changes of boyhood, I marvel at the peculiar progress of my life. How brilliant is the plan that moved me from disillusion and disgust to the playgrounds of youth! How subtle the hand that steered me from wheelchairs to marriage to games! How terrible it would be the other way around. How, I wonder, could the human race ever handle such diminution, loss, decay?

And then, as my frame fattens and shrinks, as my fingernails shrivel into tiny half moons and my ears into the most delicate shells, as people appear who hold and rock and tickle me, I am filled with increasing joy. It won't be long now! Bradley has disappeared, but it doesn't matter. Nothing matters except the changes ahead, the voyage home, when I shall kick off my booties, wriggle out of diapers and pins, and pierce the membrane that separates me from my mother's womb.

At last the day comes. There is much excitement all around but I pay no attention. I do not need them; my course is charted. And then it begins. I enter and dissolve. The warm fluid surrounds me. I start to glide upstream, propelled by spasms and waves. Gradually I dissolve into my component parts, ovum and wriggle-tailed sperm, molecules, atoms, shudders of electricity. The warm core waits and I am deconceived, unbegotten, at the very moment that I marvel for the last time at the richness of life, at the beauty of the world. And then, on the edge of eternity, I am possessed by the last necessary truths—truths that have arrived too late to be of any use: Love is eternal. Death is an illusion. Trust everyone.

The Lost Chord

Charles was introduced to the two young women during the intermission of the Philharmonic concert, the Friday evening series. He hadn't wanted to meet them. When he saw Alf Andreas waving him over he felt distinctly annoyed. He had planned to think about the music he'd just heard, especially the cadenzas. They had sounded quite un-Mozartean. He wondered if the flautist, who was elfin and came from Ireland, had written them himself.

"Charles, I want you to meet two dear friends of mine." Alf's hair had gone through many changes over the years, Charles reflected, but he had never seen it like this. It was the color of chopped liver. "This is Dr. Horn, kids."

The two women were staring at him. That wasn't anything new. He didn't mind the intense scrutiny of strangers now but when he was young it had bothered him a lot. He could hardly step into a room without all eyes turning toward him, especially after people found out he was a physician. Black doctors weren't so rare nowadays but people still stared.

"Claire and Tay are filmmakers, Charles. Just back from a fund-raising tour. What was it, kids, five cities in ten days?"

The two women had the sexless look of Boy Scouts. Short hair, scrubbed faces, no makeup. And they were wearing jeans, of course. He disapproved of jeans at the Philharmonic.

"Just four cities," said Tay. On closer inspection, Tay was shaped differently. She was slim at the shoulders but had a wide bottom. The other one was slim all the way down.

"What kind of films do you make?" His voice was light and pleasant. His tone of polite inquiry. It was a miracle, really, because he didn't care what kind of films they made. He had also intended to think about the key of C-major. A greatly underrated key.

"Historical documentaries." The answer seemed to come from a great distance away. Now he had to go to the bathroom. Would he have time? Sometimes you had to wait in line to urinate.

"Um, Charles, I hope you aren't going to be annoyed at me."

He turned sharply toward Alf. He hated remarks like that. It meant people had done something they shouldn't. "Why in the name of God should I be annoyed?"

There, he was sounding cranky already, dammit. He rolled his program into a tight cylinder. Now it would be hard to read. He thought he'd trained himself out of that.

"There's no reason you should be, Dr. Horn."

It was Tay, the one shaped like a pre-Columbian vase. "Alfred told us you made some films years ago."

"Well, he had no business telling you that."

He glared at Alf, who was now twisting and twitching with guilt. When had Alf found out about his reel? He couldn't remember. That was nothing new either.

"Now don't get all worked up, Charles, there's no reason the kids shouldn't know. They're in the business."

"We believe your films are extremely important. There are very few films of gay life in the thirties." It was the slim one, he'd forgotten her name already. Her voice was thin and piercing. It stabbed through the groups on either side of them. He thought he saw heads lift.

"There was only one film. And I made it in the forties. In the thirties I was too busy to think about such nonsense."

"Yes, Charles, you were in medical school. I told them you were very unusual."

Alf was trying to placate him but it was useless. He couldn't possibly know what it had been like in those days. What it had taken to get through the lectures, the labs, the residency. My God, any whisper, any scandal, and they'd have thrown him out on his ear. He'd have wound up back in Philadelphia, delivering letters like his father. If he'd been white he might have gotten away with some hanky-panky. God knows it went on. But they'd watched him like a hawk, all of them. Always, always, the exception.

"The forties are underdocumented too, Dr. Horn." This was the thin one, with the voice like a scalpel.

He started to speak, started to protest, but the words wouldn't come. That was another recent development. He couldn't seem to find the right words when he needed them. Now it was too late. They were flooding him with sentences, taking turns, with Alf bobbing around with extra phrases. For a moment he felt dizzy and closed his eyes. Still, he had to listen.

They were making a film about the old days. Looking for photos, people, places, memories. He heard phrases like "before Stonewall" and "subterranean roots." Followed by "public television" and "educational distribution."

He wanted to say that his reel would look pretty funny in a modern film, 8-millimeter, full of jump-cuts, all grainy and jerky and badly lit, but he couldn't find the words. Besides, they didn't give him a chance. There was something else too, something he couldn't quite find, couldn't dive down to discover, but he knew there was no point in pursuing that. It would take him hours, maybe days, to find it.

"We'd really appreciate the chance to screen your film. If you prefer, we can duplicate your original just for safety."

Now. He could do it now. "I promised someone in my film I would never show it publicly." His voice was good and strong, thank heavens. It was his authority sound, the one he had used in the hospital when his staff got rambunctious. A C-major tone, you might say.

"How do you know he'd still mind?"

"Would you ask him?"

"That was a long time ago."

Their voices just tickled his ear, like so many gnats. He wasn't going to take it back, even though it wasn't exactly true. Besides, he no longer even knew the truth about all that. He hadn't thought about it in years.

They were still tickling his ear when the chimes sounded. Now he didn't have time to go to the toilet, dammit. His prostate, swollen after years of devoted service, would give him no peace for the second half of the program. They were all staring at him. He'd probably been rude. But his frontal vein was throbbing and he couldn't stay, couldn't smooth things over. He turned away, aware of their stares, aware that they expected him to say something accommodating. But that was out of the question. He was never accommodating. If he had been, he wouldn't have made that movie in the first place.

Moving across the lobby, he tried to hold himself straight. He knew how he looked — bent over like a crab, scuttling sideways. Damn this osteoarthritis! He had to remember to pick up a fresh program too.

By the time Charles got to his seat the concertmaster was already tuning up. The other players were adjusting their strings. It was a moment that usually gave him the keenest pleasure. But tonight, thanks to the awful scene in the lobby, his mind was buzzing. Films! Gay liberation! And of course, Patrick. These matters prevented him from enjoying the preparations for the Schubert symphony coming up. He took a deep breath and closed his eyes. It was time to control himself. He'd always been proud of his self-control. Even his bowel movements had come exactly when he willed them. Now it was time to erase the unpleasantness.

And then, as if on cue, he recalled a comment made about Franz Schubert. It had been applied not to the symphony he was about to hear, but to the trio in B-flat. "It makes the world a brighter place," Robert Schumann had written. How perfect, how apt. As he reflected on the remark, Charles felt the world begin to brighten. In a few moments it would shimmer and blaze. He settled back in his seat, bathed in a new serenity. Yes, his self-control was still remarkable.

The conductor was threading his way through the basses. As he bowed to the audience, Charles recalled a comment he had discovered in the *Times* last month. One of their critics, obviously an idiot, had written that the world could never be a brighter place because of a piece of music. This was not the function of music.

Charles had been instantly furious when he read that. He'd composed an answer on his little portable at once, using his best stationery, with Charles Mathew Horn, Jr., M.D, at the top. The *Times* didn't print it of course, but he'd kept a carbon and showed it to several friends. He wasn't sure if they grasped the importance of the issue, but they had said kind things. It was really quite plain. The critic had been wrong and his error had to be corrected. Nobody had the right to let an untruth go by. It would grow and grow, like the lie Don Basilio warned about in *The Barber of Seville* — spreading conflagrations throughout the world. Charles knew that most people regarded this view of accuracy as simple and old-fashioned. His artistic friends labeled it scientific and let it go at that. But it was neither simple nor scientific. Truth was not relative. Truth was a fact, no more, no less. You had to pick your way around lies and errors the way you walked on dark streets at night — watching out for potholes and cars and muggers. If he hadn't believed in the purity, the absoluteness of truth, he'd never have been able to get through his life.

The maestro gave the downbeat. Charles sat back. his hands folded in his lap. Everything around him faded and he sank into a light drugged bliss. A C-minor haze enveloped him. It was, he thought dimly, the color of the *schlag* they used as topping for Viennese coffee. Rich, creamy and slightly indigestible. And then, as the second theme sounded, an obstacle rose to interrupt his rapture. It was a bit of memory, stirred up by the scene in the lobby. It had to do with truth. His devotion to truth was not without its pitfalls. It meant he had to rule out a great many things, stay inside a little circle of light, as it were, where everything was bright and clear. Once he had ventured outside that little circle of light. And gotten into trouble.

He turned his mind this way and that, trying to avoid the stirring of memory, but without success. It was all connected to this very symphony. He shifted his feet, annoyed at his failing concentration. And then, with a powerful effort, he wrenched free and returned to the music. He'd missed one of the sweetest modulations, one he always waited for. He was determined not to miss another one.

Yes, the world was now, incomparably, a brighter place.

When Charles got home after the concert — leaving the hall by a back exit to avoid running into Alf and his friends — he fixed himself a nightcap. He always had a drink at bedtime. As a vasodilator it was to be recommended. Except for some dental problems, he'd never been seriously ill.

He didn't turn on the radio while sipping his Scotch, not even to hear the late news. He didn't want to disturb the evening's music. The Schubert had been satisfying — not great but solid and interesting. The themes swirled in his ear. He also knew that the late news would interfere with his job, which was to track down the memory associated with the symphony. Of course, he couldn't pursue it directly. Then it would disappear forever, into the trackless wastes of his unreliable mind. He had to be careful. Also, for some reason, he had to keep himself distanced from what lay ahead, as if it were a microbe-ridden bandage that could only be handled with forceps.

He took another sip of Scotch. There. He had a clue already. Carnegie Hall. He'd still been night administrator at the hospital, having been promoted from admitting doctor only a short while before. That meant it had been a Monday. He only had Monday nights off from

1945 to 1952. That discovery deserved another sip of Scotch.

Now. Who was the conductor? Koussevitzky, Rodzinski, Toscanini, Beecham? None seemed right. There were also Fürtwangler and Weingartner but, to the best of his recollection, they had never guest-conducted here. He must look that up tomorrow.

Of course, he knew the ending of the little episode. Or part of it. He preferred not to get too far ahead of himself. Not only was ignoring sequence to fall into error but there were, well, other things involved. He certainly didn't want to review all those at this hour of the night.

Bruno Walter! The name sailed into view and he could see Dr. Walter quite clearly. An unimpressive man, slight, bespectacled, scholarly, conducting Schubert with a precise baton. And then he saw the rest of it, quite large and luminous and amazingly full of excitement.

The young man in the dark serge suit, with a crew cut, bronzed skin and astonished blue eyes, was with a pretty girl. She was his date. She had her hair falling over one eye like Veronica Lake. He himself had barely noticed them until, during intermission, he had caught the young man's glance resting on him a moment longer than necessary.

Yes, a moment longer! Was there anything to compare with the subtle signals of the old days? When you became a master of intrigue, of artifice, when the thrill of making contact despite danger everywhere added spice to the chase? No wonder spy novels were so popular nowadays. Everybody needed some excitement in their lives. In those days, with stories about the Homintern in *Life* and *Time* (and could anyone today understand how Henry Luce's hatreds had set the tone of the period?), you couldn't be too careful. Even now, sitting in his apartment on West 83rd Street, he noted a slight gastric discharge in his stomach. His body fluids still responded to old cues, to signals of four decades ago!

Yes, the young man had given him one look and then another. The second more significant. The girl with the Veronica Lake hairdo was talking very fast; phrases about Mt. Holyoke and Waltz Evenings arched over to Charles. *I'm stuck*, that blue glance said, *it's up to you.*

And then he'd had his inspiration. It had come to him with the silken ease of a Schubert modulation.

He'd gone to the velvet balustrade and placed his program on it. Then he'd taken out his Waterman's, uncapped it with a flourish, and written alongside the tempo markings for the Schubert symphony which Dr. Walter had just conducted so elegantly. He kept watch on the young man out of the corner of his eye. He had positioned himself so that his girlfriend's back was to Charles. He was watching. After finishing, Charles had closed the program and walked off. The whole thing only took thirty seconds.

The young man quickly found an excuse to move. His girlfriend was watching and he had to do it quickly, deftly. And he had. His own program was at the ready; the switch was accomplished in a flash. She hadn't seen a thing. A few minutes later he led her to their seat in the front row. Charles had watched, his heart hammering, his respiration shallow. The second half of the program had blazed with extra brilliance, not only because Dr. Walter was in charge but because Charles knew with a certainty beyond all doubt that the young man would soon be in his arms. It had been, he thought now, finishing his Scotch, a song without words—*ein Leid ohne Worte*—just as Mendelssohn (not his favorite composer) had created.

His phone had rung around midnight that very night. He didn't even bother with the usual formalities. "How did you like the Schubert?" he had said into the receiver as soon as he picked up.

"I thought it was slick," came the eager voice at the other end.

He resisted the idea of another highball before bedtime. It would provoke unpleasant action in his bladder while he slept. Besides, more liquor might shorten the necessary distance between himself and the memories he had unearthed. He certainly didn't want to wallow around in the past. Not *that* past, anyway. Damn! How he wished he hadn't run into Alf Andreas tonight.

It took him almost an extra hour to compose his mind for sleep, even after turning out the light.

The morning after the concert, Charles had his usual breakfast of tea and unsweetened granola. Then he read the paper, which had been delivered, reading first the music reviews and then checking his stocks. During this he listened to the morning music show on the classical station. The single large room in which he lived—had lived for forty years—was sparsely furnished. When friends asked him why he didn't buy extra chairs or a big sofa he replied that he had furnished his home with music and didn't need anything else. It was true. The big Gulbransen piano, the stereo equipment, the bookcases for his records and scores, took up half the available space.

He looked around the room critically. There was dust here and there. He hadn't been keeping up with things, connected no doubt to his recent shortness of breath. The winter months were always hardest. He should have bought a place in Puerto Rico years ago. He'd gone down there intending to do just that, while prices were still reasonable, but on his third day he'd switched on his portable radio and heard a large, mixed chorus singing the Grieg Piano Concerto in Spanish. It had ruined Puerto Rico for good—unfairly, no doubt, since the Casals Festival was admirable, but he couldn't help himself. And now he was stuck in New York. He couldn't afford to buy a winter home. His pension hadn't kept up with inflation.

The phone rang just as the announcer introduced a Beethoven piano sonata, one of his favorites, the Opus 31, No. 3. A pity. But he answered without a show of impatience. "This is Dr. Horn speaking."

The voice at the other end slipped into his brain like the thin edge of a knife. "Dr. Horn, this is Claire Bridgman. From last night, remember?"

"I remember your first name. To the best of my recollection you did not mention your family name."

There was a pause at the other end. No doubt she didn't like being corrected. No one did. But he couldn't let inaccuracy slip by. "Um, I'm calling to invite you to a little presentation we're having. Alf said you might like to come."

"How did Alf know that?"

"He didn't know, he just hoped." Her voice sharpened, as if she'd just honed it on flint. Yes, she was irritated. "It's about our work."

Their film project. He'd seen that coming. There was going to be a lecture at a public school downtown. She wanted him to come. "We'll be giving a progress report. We'll also be showing preliminary documentation on some people you might have known personally." She mentioned some famous names.

Of course, they all thought that if you were over a certain age you knew all the other people who were alive at the same time. Why in God's name should he have known Bill Tilden or Djuna Barnes or Lauritz Melchior? They might as well have asked him if he knew Oscar Wilde. It had taken all his wits just to remember the names of his hospital staff, especially after he became medical superintendent.

"Are you there, Dr. Horn?"

"Call me Charles, please."

Her voice sweetened. "Will you come, Charles? We'll be glad to comp you in."

After he hung up he regretted having accepted. It was obvious they were trying to pry his reel out of him. He went back to his chair feeling slightly dizzy. He didn't like the whole thing. Not at all. In fact, he had the brief image of a monster that had been awakened from the sleep of centuries. But that was ridiculous. There was nothing about his life, his past, that could not be examined in daylight. He glanced at the clock. It was nine-fifteen, time for his bowel movement. He would have to forgo the rest of the Beethoven sonata. After he finished, he would dust.

It was while he was dusting that he came face-to-face with his film library. He wasn't sure exactly how, but suddenly he found himself inside the hall closet, staring at the cans that were neatly stacked on the third shelf, each with a bit of adhesive for titling. He didn't really remember opening the closet door, but here he was. He flicked his rag over the tops and sides. The titles—his lettering had always been bold and neat—jumped out at him. DALMATIAN COAST. FJORD CRUISE ON S.S. HEDREN. VERONA OPERA. SANTA SOFIA AND BLUE MOSQUE. His eye skittered over them, looking for something else. There it was, at the bottom. It hadn't been removed for years. PATRICK. Followed by the dates. Funny how long ago that was, even though it still seemed very recent to him.

His fingers seemed to have a life of their own, touching, then skimming the flat, round tin. Now they were lifting, pulling. Now the dustcloth was dropped, forgotten, and he was propelled slowly toward his chair, the can under his arm, his dizziness combining with his shortness of breath to make it imperative that he sit down. He shouldn't be doing this, shouldn't be interrupting his dusting, his morning routine. It was a bad sign, of a piece with his concentration lapses during the concert last night, his poor sleep, his slight dyspnea. What would happen if he lost control of himself for good?

And then he forgot all that as he suddenly recalled how Patrick had looked as he stepped inside his door—this very door—the morning after the Carnegie Hall concert. He'd been wearing a loafer coat, oxford shirt, khaki pants, buckskins. Also a necktie. Everybody wore neckties in those days. But his wide-set blue eyes had been his most remarkable feature.

It seemed they had hardly talked at all before they were holding each other. Patrick didn't want a cup of coffee or a beer. Patrick only wanted him.

It was amazing how many people had found him attractive. He'd never been handsome — short, dark, compact, with a round head and pushed-in features. But the pretty boys had liked him, considered him sexy, wanted to go to bed with him. He was exotic, of course. He appealed to their curiosity, their sense of the forbidden. But above all, he was a lusty man and they had sensed it. Smelled his virility the way you could smell money or class or power.

It certainly hadn't taken them long, that first morning, to move to the little sleeping alcove. The most appealing thing about Patrick, aside from his flawless skin and firm ass, had been those glorious blue eyes. Charles thought he had never seen such jeweled eyes, not even when he was growing up and had gotten a crush on one white boy after another. Yes, it had always been white boys and now Patrick McRae, whose skin looked as if it had snowed on him during the night, was in his arms and not averse to having his eyes kissed. It had been the culmination of a grand adventure, an adventure tinged with daring and quick-wittedness, and they had laughed at it even as they cavorted in bed. But it had been their conversation afterward, the first of many, that had changed everything.

They were lying on the little studio couch, smoking Players cigarettes. His hand was resting on Patrick's chest, almost burning with its pale fire, when Patrick told him, quite casually between puffs, that he was a student at Juilliard. He was studying piano.

"You're going to be a concert pianist?" Charles' voice had crept upward as he asked. The young man next to him, his ridged chest under his hand, seemed to have changed into someone else entirely.

"Yeah." He mentioned his teacher, a celebrated virtuoso. Charles had heard this man play — once, in fact, with Toscanini. This man sometimes called Patrick at eight in the morning, just to make sure he got up early to practice.

Patrick giggled. "He's gonna be teed off 'cause I'm not home this morning. I've got a lesson tomorrow." Patrick looked up at Charles, waiting for his eyes to be kissed again.

But Charles had not been able to respond. A musician! He had a musician in his arms! He'd wanted to be a musician himself, had realized it the first time he walked into the Abyssinian Baptist Church with his parents and heard the choir and the soloists. The men, he knew right away, were singing purple and the ladies gold. He'd tried to tell his mother this but she had hushed him up. Later he'd heard one of the soloists referred to as Frying Pan Bill. He'd known without being told where he got that name—because he was round and black and had a voice like cast-iron. He'd tried to tell his mother this too, but she hadn't understood. She had never understood, nor had his father, who was determined he should be a doctor.

Yes, his dream of music had been hopeless, right from the beginning. He never even had time to take a music course. Keeping his scholarship to Haverford, being admitted to Columbia, then the nightmarish residency at St. Luke's—no time, no time for anything but medicine. For books and cadavers and Gray's *Anatomy* and grand rounds. But he'd listened. God, how he had listened! Sometimes, when things got bad, he would go to his room and turn on his little Philco and lie there, not stirring, for hours. Just soak in the sound, the solace. He'd never have gotten through all that loneliness and fatigue and bigotry if he hadn't had that little cathedral of music next to his bed.

He had told Patrick this, little by little, over their next few meetings. It had come out of him slowly, shyly, as they lay in bed, or had their breakfasts of ham and eggs. He had never admitted so much to anyone else. It had always been too private, too filled with loss or misunderstanding. But Patrick, with his truth-seeking blue eyes, had grasped it right away. "You're really a musician, Charlie"—he had always called him Charlie, in spite of requests not to—"and you got sidetracked into doctoring." And then he would stare at Charles, examining him with blue spotlights. He had never, Charles thought, been seen so clearly.

It was at their fourth meeting that Patrick had made his remarkable offer. It had come as Charles was pouring coffee. The bed in the alcove was still unmade.

"You know what, Charlie? I'm going to give you music lessons." Patrick was wearing just a bath towel. Drops of water sparkled on his snowy skin; he looked as if he had bathed in diamonds.

Charles had laughed. It was out of the question. He didn't have time. He was still on night-duty. He was taking a course in hospital administration. Sometimes he came home and fell into bed, he was so tired.

But Patrick wouldn't be put off. He began to make plans, name books, courses. They would start with harmony and counterpoint. Exercises in figured bass. This could be done without a piano.

Now, seated in his armchair, the can of film in his lap, Charles marveled at the offer, at Patrick's insistence. How kind he had been, how sweet with the juices of life! His eye went to one of his bookcases. The thick blue volume was right there. He'd bought it at G. Schirmer's, *Harmony* by Walter Piston, Professor of Music at Harvard. A revised edition had been published that very year. Patrick had said they would start at Chapter One and go right through.

Charles couldn't help smiling as he remembered. Chapter One was Scales and Intervals. In those days he didn't even know what a scale was, really, to say nothing of dominants, subdominants, diminished chords and augmentations. But he had learned, dammit, he had learned. Patrick had turned up twice a week in this very room, arranging his schedule to suit Charles', his satchel full of the concertos he was learning. And he had gone over Charles' childish exercises, correcting, encouraging, illustrating. And gradually Charles had come to understand the vast and intricate world of sound, learned its history and structure, the innovations of the great composers. And when the time had come to buy a piano, he had made the rounds of the dealers. Four hundred dollars for the Gulbransen represented a small fortune back then, but he had plunked down the money.

The can of film felt warm and heavy against his thighs. Those months that followed—almost a year, really—had been the most remarkable of his life. He had expanded his definition of truth. He had moved out of his hard bright circle of light, his focus of ascertainable fact, and onto the dim stages of uncertainty. He knew he was taking a chance in doing so. Exposing himself to the great unanswerable questions of why and what-if and do you suppose. Sometimes, in bad moments, he imagined that these questions were towering over him and that just behind them were thousands of others, stretching as far as the eye could see. For example, why had he let his parents push him into medicine when he'd known right along he wanted to be a musician? What if he and Patrick were to set up house together? Do you suppose they would spend the rest of their lives together?

But in his good moments these questions didn't bother him. In fact, they didn't even seem like questions at all. Because they were both very happy. His film, in fact, had been started as a record of their happiness—at the piano and over coffee and, yes, even in bed. Thanks to the self-timer he'd been able to capture not just their singleness but their doubleness, black and white, serious and giddy, dressed and un-dressed. Of course, he'd had to develop his negative himself. Right over there next to the kitchen, he'd curtained off a little darkroom, learning all about the solutions and developers and printers. Eastman Kodak would never have sent him back a print—the negative would have come back from Rochester with a little tag, "Not suitable for development."

Patrick preferred to spend time with him here, in this apartment. Although Charles suggested concerts, trips, it was never possible. Either Patrick had a lesson or had to practice or go to his job in the school library. And he, of course, had his duties at the hospital.

He stirred suddenly and moved the film from his lap to the side-table. Patrick's reluctance to meet him outside should have warned him, should have signaled that something was not true. But he'd been blind. Blind to the danger of stepping outside his circle of light.

What an idiot he had been—what a child!

The film conference was to be held in a public school in the Village. Charles took the subway. It taxed his strength more than usual. He found the stairs steeper, the noise louder, the vibration of the train more jarring. At several points his mild dyspnea returned—a short-ness of breath that, if he hadn't known better, he would have associ-ated with the first warnings of cardiac arrest. By the time he got to the school entrance, he was exhausted. He hoped they remembered to save a seat for him—the place was packed.

"We have a comp for you, Dr. Horn."

The girl at the door had spotted him. Well, that wasn't hard to do.

"I told Miss . . . Miss . . ." He'd forgotten her name, dammit.

"Claire?"

"Yes. Claire. I told her I expected to pay."

She didn't seem to hear. She stamped a ticket on the back and hand-ed it to him. Several young people passed him, dressed in what looked like camping attire. He hadn't seen so many knapsacks in one place since Abercrombie & Fitch closed their store on Madison Avenue. "John will show you to your seat," she said.

A tall, slender young man materialized at his side. He led Charles down the aisle. Charles wanted to speak, tried to speak, but couldn't think what to say. While he was still fumbling around in his mind the young man spoke. "Are you the one with the old porno film?" He looked down at Charles and flashed his teeth.

Charles couldn't believe his ears. "What did you say?" His voice was louder than he'd intended. "Would you repeat that, please?"

"Gee, I'm sorry." The young man didn't look sorry at all. "Claire and Tay said you were, like, a pioneer."

"I do not make pornographic films." His voice boomed up and down the aisle.

The young man shrugged. "Well okay."

They were at his seat, thank God. He reached out to grab the back of the chair. The young man helped him. "Enjoy it," he said, just before rushing off.

Charles sat frozen, pressing his hand against the pulse in his forehead. It was Alf, of course. Alf had told them he made pornography. How could he do that? It wasn't true. He'd filmed certain . . . well, intimate moments, between Patrick and himself. Moments that were rare and beautiful. But not pornography. He'd have to speak to the girls right after the lecture, tell them they'd been misinformed. He'd never shot a foot of dirt in his life.

Without warning, the lights went off. The hubbub lessened. Some people filed onto the stage, among them Claire and Tay. Claire's eyes swept across the first few rows of seats, resting on him for a moment. He had the uncomfortable feeling that she was making sure he'd arrived.

After some introductions, one of the men moved to the lectern. He was young and coffee-colored, his hair puffed out in a natural Afro. He was going to present a slide-show. He had collected visuals from World War II—drag shows on Pacific atolls, all-male dancing at the U.S.O., lesbian entrapments and trials, V.D. leaflets and warnings about red-light districts. Charles listened carefully. He remembered many of the pictures from *Life* magazine, had studied them when they first came out, trying to fit their warnings into what he knew about himself. He had never dreamed that he would be sitting, forty years later, viewing them as artifacts from an unenlightened age.

"One of the great untold stories of the period concerns the fraternization and love between black men and white men." Where had that remark come from? It seemed to have nothing to do with the slide-show just concluded. And the houselights had been turned up slightly.

Charles had the uneasy feeling that this part of the show was for his benefit.

"Although the armed services were segregated, reflecting the society around them, there were many instances of men and women overcoming race barriers. We hope to include old, rare footage which our research has turned up, illustrating the fact that gay love transcended bigotry."

The speaker was looking directly at him. Charles felt his flesh chill. What in the name of God was going on?

"We have been only partly successful in reassuring older gays that there is no danger in opening their closet doors, that their experience is part of our heritage."

There was a murmur of assent around the auditorium, then the patter of applause. The youngsters around him liked these noble sentiments. They seemed to be under the impression that the past, *his* past, belonged to them.

The speaker concluded his remarks, keeping his eyes fixed on Charles, whose respiration had speeded up unpleasantly. When he returned to his seat, Claire and Tay swept Charles with their eyes. He refused to meet their gaze, just sat and stared stonily ahead. How simple it seemed to them! As if they had broken off a piece of the truth and could flash it on a screen! But truth—the truth of the past— wasn't as available as they thought. *Love between black men and white men.* Did the speaker, who had probably been in diapers when Martin Luther King was shot, really understand what it had been like?

Claire had moved to the lectern. She was talking about budgets and contributions. Charles didn't listen. His mind had twisted back, out of control, to the concert. Patrick's concert at Lewisohn Stadium, one of the summer series which introduced promising new pianists to the New York public. Funny how he hadn't thought about it in years, had allowed it to lie buried, the way the can of film had been buried under the trips to Norway and Turkey and Italy. But now the summer evening slipped out from under its burden, the weight of other memories, and moved across the screen of his mind.

He had seen the notice in the Sunday *Times*. It wasn't large, and the name of Patrick McRae was even smaller—tucked at the bottom of the ad. He would play the Rachmaninoff Second on a Tuesday evening in August. Charles suddenly recalled the name of the conductor — Hootstratten, a Dutchman. He had a showy baton style and wiggled his bottom in time to the music.

But that wasn't the important thing. He was rambling. He must get to the point. Patrick hadn't mentioned the concert to him. His New York debut. He should have known, from that little fact, that something was wrong. That the truth he had glimpsed behind the clear jewelry of Patrick's eyes, was incomplete. Or, God help him, not even truth at all. But he hadn't known, hadn't been warned. And so he had put on his seersucker suit, rolled up his umbrella (hints of rain) and taken the IRT uptown express. The crowds filing into the stadium had seemed happy and good-natured. But perhaps they only reflected the way he felt. He was going to see and hear Patrick play in public! He was going to share in the acclaim tendered the young man he had met in a daring maneuver at Carnegie Hall. Patrick's coming triumph would be his too.

Hootstratten had conducted some Tchaikowski first — a poor choice, sentimentally played. Romeo and Juliet couldn't have been so full of self-pity. But it didn't matter. All that mattered was the way Patrick looked in a white suit, a stain of snow against the piano as he took his bow, and how he would play. Charles was aware of his own palms sweating, his fingers trembling. He knew the opening chords by heart, had studied them, parsed them with Patrick. And now, here they were . . . the sound, thick as impasto on a canvas, rolling around the huge arena. He was off and running!

Charles sat without moving as the florid music filled the night. Patrick's hands leaped around the keyboard, stabbing chords into life, taking chances on the runs, leaning into the cadenzas as if he were driving a motorcycle. The music showered, blazed, subsided. At the end, Charles slumped on the stone bench, exhausted. He felt as if he had played every note himself.

He didn't join in the cheers and applause. He didn't have the strength. He just sat quietly, a slight smile on his young lips, aware that they had done it. He and Patrick had done it. And then, quite softly, his eyes had begun to drip. The ducts had been stimulated by something quite beyond his control — a neurokinesthesic maneuver up there on the stage — and he was immobilized under the night sky at 138th Street. It seemed that all his life, since he had first heard the church choir singing in purple and gold, had been a preparation for this moment.

He'd wanted to rush backstage at intermission, but restrained himself. It was too soon, and they probably wouldn't let him through anyway. He'd sat through the Mahler First impatiently. The climax of the evening was yet to come.

The press of people backstage had not been great. Patrick had been standing amid a clump of instrument cases, easy to pick out in his white suit against the black leather. He was talking to a grey-haired gentleman accompanied by his wife. Charles had no trouble recognizing this gentleman. He was Patrick's teacher, the famous virtuoso who had played with Toscanini. It was a stroke of luck. He'd be able to tell the virtuoso how much he admired his playing.

He stood very still, a few feet away. In another moment the truth of their relationship would be mirrored in those blue eyes.

And that was the way it happened, more or less. Patrick did look up, did see him, but what was reflected in his eyes was not the truth that Charles expected. Not the truth of welcome and sharing. If Charles had had to name it, he would have said it was the truth of shock and fear. Not that he glimpsed this all at once. No. It came to him over the weeks and months as he thought about what had happened next. Patrick, on seeing him, did not stir. His gaze returned to his teacher, who was now saying goodbye. Someone else turned up, a relative from the sound of the kisses and talk, and still Patrick didn't move. Charles, standing ramrod-straight, his umbrella neatly furled and hooked on the sleeve of his seersucker jacket, looked neither right nor left. A terrible cold had seized his solar plexus. He couldn't move either, not in any direction. He seemed to be frozen in space and time—between the well-wishers around him and the pressing figures of his childhood, including his mother and father, who had warned him about situations like this when they kept insisting he should be a doctor.

And then, at last, Patrick had come over. He had shaken hands nervously with Charles and thanked him for coming. It was all polite and friendly but it was not what Charles had expected when he rode uptown on the subway nor when he had wept under the faint stars of upper Manhattan. It was not the truth as he understood it. The worst part was that he had continued to smile throughout. He hadn't been able to get rid of the smile until he was alone in his own apartment.

Claire had ended her talk without his having noticed. People were getting up. He waited a few moments then rose. He moved stiffly up the aisle. They were waiting for him at the top.

"Charles, this is Matt Dawkins." Claire was introducing him to the boy who had talked about World War II. Charles was aware of the usual intense scrutiny. He thought about telling Matt Dawkins that if he was searching for his heritage he wouldn't find it here. At least not the simple truth he had set himself to find. But when Matt said, in his pleasant voice, "Can we talk?" he only replied, "Not now."

"Matt is going to call you." Claire's voice was loud and bossy. Charles started to say this was out of the question when Matt said softly, "I'd just like to talk with you, Charles," and Charles knew he would probably let the young man visit him. "What you can do right now," he said finally, "is find me a taxicab."

He tried to control his thoughts on the ride uptown but they kept sliding away from him. Patrick seemed to be sharing the dark space beside him. He had not seen his teacher-lover after the concert. Patrick had called many times but Charles had been firm. No, he didn't want a lesson today. No, he didn't want Patrick to go over his canons and fughettas. Sorry, he was busy at the hospital. Patrick had reacted in various ways. None of them had any effect on Charles, who was trying to work out some things in his mind.

He had fallen into error. He had never really shared Patrick's life, never shared anything but sex and music. That had been a great deal but it had not been enough. Perhaps he had been nothing more than Patrick's backstreet stud.

When he first realized this, he'd been sitting at his piano. The next moment he had felt a fierce shrinking inside his skull. The spotlight which had been playing for a year over a very large area, an area unlit in his life until then, now narrowed its focus. He was aware only of his hands on the keys, the bulk of the piano, the single room in which he lived. Everything in this area was bright and clear. Outside, however, there was nothing but sadness and danger and dusk.

There had been only one serious temptation after that. Patrick had turned up at his door. Rung the bell at their usual hour—eight in the morning. The thought of Patrick standing there, a satchel of scores under his arm, his angel eyes pleading for forgiveness, was almost too much for Charles. He had imagined what he might do—slam Patrick around the room, shout out his anger, fight for what he wanted. But he had not. He had not let him in. He had stayed inside his circle of light, alone.

And so, with his marvelous self-control, he had willed a new life for himself. The first step had been to put away his exercises, those childish scribbles of clefs and notes and flats and sharps. It was too late to be a composer or performer. He would have to remain what he'd been all along, an appreciator of music. That capacity had increased, thanks to his studies of the last year, but there was no reason to think he could become a professional. It was not his truth.

The second step had been to refurbish his career. He had slackened off, gotten careless. All that would change now. And it had. He'd soon been promoted from night administrator to general assistant, then to deputy administrator. The other bureaucrats had sensed the change in him, seen that his steadiness, his self-discipline, had been obscured for a while but had now reemerged. In time he'd risen to the top of his profession. He had made people respect him; he had made some of them afraid of him. He had become famous for being tough.

The third step had been the hardest. He had trained himself not to expect too much. Oh, he'd had a good life—money, position, travel, this comfortable apartment. He'd had plenty of music, and sex when he needed it. But at one time he had hoped for more. That too, he had come to realize, was not his truth.

After arriving home from the lecture in the Village, Charles sat for a long time over his nightcap. The film was still on the side-table, where he had left it a few days ago. At first he had thought he would screen it, for old-time's sake, but now he knew he would not. Tomorrow he would put it back in the closet.

At last, aware that his respiration was rapid and that he was experiencing slight chest pain, he moved to his little sleeping alcove. The studio bed on which he had entertained Patrick had been replaced long ago by a platform with a water mattress. He stretched out, first removing his glasses and putting them on the night-table. In a moment, when he felt stronger, he would undress.

And then, although the apartment was silent, he heard very clearly the opening chords of the Rachmaninoff concerto, just as Patrick had played them so many years ago. The sound was both thick and transparent, like glaze upon glaze in an old painting, and he listened with mingled shock and pleasure. The next moment, as the orchestra swung into its big C-minor figure, he knew what he would do. He would let them have the film. Let them have it even though it would be used to signify something that had not been true, that would, in fact, grow and grow in falsehood like the lie Don Basilio warned about in *The Barber of Seville*. And then, as the pain in his chest increased, a new thought came to him. It was possible, just barely possible, that the film, though used untruthfully, would have some value. It might inspire someone to demand more, fight harder, claim justice. Perhaps—and this was his last thought as the jolt stung him and he understood quite clearly what was coming—it would keep some other young man from spending an entire life inside a tiny, imprisoning, circle of light.

A Rose in Murcia

He should not have come. He knew it as soon as he boarded the rat-
tletrap bus in Palma. The realization grew as the yellow contraption
wheezed up the narrow road, over the rocks broken into pebbles by
generations of Mallorcan road gangs, past the monastery where
Chopin had spent that awful winter with George Sand. Why was he
here, jolted, parched, the scene just ended with Alex heavy on his
conscience? What did he hope to discover?

The bus heaved and groaned along the mountain road, the shifts of
gear sounding like the cry of a doomed man. Every so often the hills to
the left fell away and Frady glimpsed the Mediterranean, an azure
blur to the horizon. Alex was probably sitting over a cup of coffee on
the Borne now, his kind, seamed face under the grizzled hair showing
signs of hurt and confusion. Because Frady had insisted on making
this trip alone.

Well, he couldn't help it. He didn't want Alex with him. He didn't
want to share this detour into the past. It belonged to him alone.

The gearshift gave another tortured cry and Frady glanced to his
left. Far below, a promontory of rocks jutted into the sea. He remembered that tumble of weird shapes. They had gone fishing for bream
there, he and Tom and a new British friend named Nigel. They had
no proper equipment, just sticks and string and bread, and spent most
of the morning staring into the water at the motionless fish, which
looked delicious. Finally they had given up and scrambled across the
rocks, up through the stands of olive and umbrella pine, shouting
poetry, chasing sheep, stuffing huge pinecones into their knapsacks.
They had reached the road, the very road he was now on, sweaty and
exhilarated and hardly out of breath.

Yes, Frady thought, as the bus rounded the last curve and the little village came into view—hardly out of breath. The phrase signaled the difference between past and present as well as anything. He glanced down at his hands, noting the liver spots struggling faintly to the surface. The stains of age. He'd probably have trouble now even walking up from the beach, much less chasing sheep and shouting poetry.

The houses of brown fieldstone were coming into view now, basking like lizards in the morning sun. Above, on a rise under the Teix, the curtain of mountains that cut off the village from the rest of the island, he saw the town itself, with its little church topped with red tiles. How he had detested that church, and the priest who had looked at him and Tom as if they were carriers of heresy or corruption. When they had arrived, after a chill sea crossing, the church had been surrounded by white blossoms, the hill bright with the plumage of the flowering almond trees. He had said to Tom that they were bridal bouquets for their own wedding, but Tom hadn't been amused.

The bus creaked to a halt. Frady stood up, aware that his heart was beating rapidly. He thought again of Alex, who had been fading during the last few minutes until he was quite dim. Well, there was no need to feel guilty. There were plenty of things Alex could do today—visit Bellver Castle, buy presents for his kids, read that history of Mallorca. But even that no longer seemed important. Now, here, in this village with its powerful freight of memory, Alex's feelings could be ignored.

As he stepped off the bus into the dusty street, everything seemed instantly familiar—the salt cod and dried beanpods in crates in front of the little grocery, the boys in short pants kicking a football, the café with its patrons in corduroy suits and berets. He might, he thought, walk in any direction and see familiar sights. Every lane, every house, would yield some richness, some association, as if the last twenty years hadn't passed, as if he were still living here with Tom.

The sound of sheep bells caught his ear. Across the street some ewes were grazing. Nearby a young shepherd rested under a tree. The Biblical scene was still enchanting. He recalled that he and Tom had stood right here, their luggage beside them, and taken in the rocky pastures, the mountains, the sheep. It seemed they had stepped into a simpler era, far from their own harsh country, where they might be truly free.

Free! The juvenile thought tolled him back to himself and he passed his hand over his forehead. He was no longer the young man who had moved here with Tom Peniman. If the nostalgia started building up again he'd have to remind himself of that. Many years had gone by—half his adult life.

Besides, he and Alex had a good present. Why should he want to wallow around in the past? "A last great autumnal passion," he had joked after they'd met at a bar in Chelsea and started spending weekends together. He'd been thinking of Zhivago and Lara—it had seemed a silly but suitable image. There was only one hitch. It hadn't been a great passion, hadn't triggered the wild abandon described by Pasternak. There had been only, well, the present, which consisted of walks and meals and movies. And sex on Saturday night—nice sex, considerate sex, but not the kind that made the earth move. At first they had talked of living together but gradually, as they entered the third, fourth and fifth years of their relationship, they had dropped the idea. Nowadays they never even referred to it. It seemed to each, though they never discussed it, an invasion of privacy.

There was the path down to the house. His eye had picked it out from all the other paths leading from the town square. How well he knew that path! Several times the pebbles had slipped under him and he'd fallen on his ass. Once he'd broken a liter of *vino tinto* and some dogs had appeared to lick it up. Tom had been furious; they'd been living on a few pesetas a day.

Frady giggled slightly as he headed toward the path. How strange and distant seemed their poverty now. They'd both quit jobs to come here—Tom as a management trainee at IBM, himself as a teacher in the New York City school system. They wanted their savings—what had it been, a thousand dollars?—to last. They had chosen Mallorca, the cheapest corner of Europe. Their house in this town cost them twenty-five dollars a month.

He was on the path now, keeping an eye out for moving pebbles. His heart was still beating a crisp tattoo. The next few minutes seemed terribly important, as if he were in the theater and the curtain was about to go up.

That sound. What was it? Keeping his eye on his feet, he tried to place it. And then, as if a dam had burst, it crashed into his consciousness. *El torrente*—of course! The stream that ran through the center of the village, bringing water down from the Teix, supplying irrigation, drink for the animals, laundromat service. And there they were, the women rinsing clothes under the pink oleander. Of course, these must be the daughters of the women he and Tom had known. Still, they looked the same—the same dresses of grey worsted, long aprons, sturdy arms, reddened hands. The same harsh appraising stares, too. He wanted to speak to them, wanted to rush over and say how glad he was to be here, but he checked himself. After he waved, one of the women nodded slightly. She was the one wearing rubber gloves.

Suddenly he remembered something that had happened here under the oleander. He had brought Tom out and posed him against the stream. He'd wanted to capture the whole thing in watercolors—the crystal torrent, the wicker panniers, the bent women, Tom with his straw peasant hat, his jutting chin, his trim and sturdy 30-year-old body. He'd painted for a bit, then they'd gone back to the house for lunch. But when he returned he found his water tumbler spilled across the page and the women gone.

The injustice of that moment returned to him. The women hadn't liked being painted, hadn't liked being picturesque for tourists. Or was it something else—the idea of one man painting another? He didn't know, then or now, but it had reminded them both of the fragility of their lives, the bare tolerance which permitted them to live undisturbed. They had both been depressed after the incident, the freedom which they had come so far to find suddenly threatened. They had gotten drunk and gone to bed hanging onto each other like life preservers. Now, crossing the little bridge over the stream, he recalled how exposed and exhausted he had often felt here. They were the only male couple for miles around. Sometimes he would become unnerved by the stares of the villagers, suddenly self-conscious about his clothes, his foreignness, his shared life—and head back to the house in panic. Yearning for the sight of Tom, the privacy of their garden. In his present nostalgia he'd forgotten all the bad things—their fishtank existence, the pointing children, the whispers.

How different things were now in New York. He and Alex knew dozens of couples just like themselves. They went to movies and plays depicting relationships like theirs; they read books and attended panel discussions on how to improve their lives. The problem wasn't too much tension but not enough. Sometimes they went out looking for excitement—in a backroom bar, a park, a porno movie. With all that in his life, why should he be nostalgic about a few months in this backwater?

The next moment, it was as if the question had never occurred to him. He'd seen the stone pillar with the tile inset that marked the entrance to the house. The words on the tile, *Mon Repos*, were almost unreadable now, but it didn't matter. The sight made his head throb. He could see the gable of the house projecting over the foliage. It seemed that the play he had come to attend had finally begun.

The gate was rusty, the lock decayed, but the shrubs along the path were clipped and the patches of margaritas well-tended. The *níspero* tree and the date palm were thriving.

There it was. The sturdy two-story house of fieldstone and mortar, trimmed in blue. Built to last for several centuries of mild Mallorcan weather. They'd first glimpsed it on a gorgeous February day, standing right on this flagstone path. Each had known instantly, without speaking, that it was what they'd been looking for. After the rental agent had unlocked the front door, they'd raced through the dark rooms with their heavy Córdoban furniture, sharing their excitement with their eyes only. They'd taken it on the spot, written out travelers' checks for six months' rent in advance. That very afternoon they'd moved in. "Mon Repos!" they had shouted in the echoing chambers as they ran around that first afternoon, "Mon Repos!" That night, after a meal that had been a disaster, they had made wild, joyous love in the bedroom upstairs, both uncontainable with joy, lust, faith in their destiny. Even now he felt faint stirrings at the memory of that first night.

Frady searched the facade for the bedroom window. There it was, last one on the right. And then, just as he turned around to view the garden behind him, he thought he saw a curtain twitch. Not in their bedroom but at the other end of the house.

He looked back quickly but the curtains were still. It must have been a trick of his peripheral vision. But he stood for a long moment, waiting, before he gave his attention to the garden.

This garden had been their first living room. On the blue bench right there they had had their best talks, made their happiest plans. He could almost see Tom now, his wiry body wrapped in scarves and sweaters, bent over his newly acquired guitar, trying to teach himself the chords with fingers that were chilled.

A brief jab of pain went through him. He didn't even know where Tom was now. Somewhere in the far east. They no longer wrote, no longer took each other along on their voyages—if only in imagination. The bond had been broken, the bond they expected to last all their lives.

They had been greatly loving toward one another. Their love had burnished this house and garden, the dark rooms and ill-equipped kitchen, the *níspero* and date palm and margaritas. Everything had absorbed and reflected their affection. And the townspeople and foreign residents, for all their stares and whispers, acknowledged their doubleness. They were described, accepted, invited, as a pair. It was always "Frady and Tom" or "Tom and Frady." They seemed to share one long, variable, triple-jointed name.

One night, coming home from a musical evening at the Petersons, an artistic American couple who lived on the main street, they had slipped and slithered down the pebbly path until suddenly they had heard a miraculous sound. It was a music more subtle, more romantic, than the Chopin and Schumann played earlier on the Peterson's rheumy piano. It was, in fact, a song of such crystal perfection that they had stopped and listened. And then, as they stared at each other— Tom's bony face silver-plated in the moonlight—they had come to the realization at the same instant. "It's a nightingale," Tom had whispered. "Yes, yes," Frady had replied in the same breath.

Though neither had ever heard a nightingale before, the song seemed to preexist in them, an unplayed music waiting for the right moment to sound. As they stood there, not stirring, the hidden bird trembling out its tune, it seemd to Frady that he was now full of the very elixir of life. To be with Tom while a nightingale's song filled the Mallorcan night was to be fully alive. It was as if an old promise had finally been kept. When the song stopped they had picked their way across the pebbles to the stone house. They hadn't said much as they got ready for bed. And the next day they had both hummed snatches of old tunes and songs, hardly aware that they were trying to duplicate, in a foolish way, the song of the nightingale.

Frady moved to the blue bench at the back of the garden and sat down. Suddenly he realized that from the moment he and Alex had planned this trip, its sole purpose was to come here to this house, to this garden, alone. It was a purpose kept hidden from Alex and, in some ways, from himself. But it had been there all along, stowed in the luggage with his underwear, in his pocket with his passport. He was coming here to find Tom, to find his joy in Tom—and it had nothing to do with the present. He shook his head slowly, appalled at the trick he had played on himself. He wanted to relive their life together, restore the old bond. It was absurd.

Their sojourn in Mallorca had been followed by several months in Paris and then home. They had arrived in New York almost broke, without job prospects, with long hair and scraggly beards. They had moved into a seedy hotel on Eighth Street. As in Mallorca and Paris, they spent long hours in cafés, cheap eateries, the barely-furnished apartments of new acquaintances. New York from this angle was not the sane, orderly place they had inhabited before going to Europe. Now it was in the grip of the flower children, the Beats, the drug explosion. They dabbled in these experiences, determined not to succumb to the forces of repression that had driven them to Spain in the first place. But it was a losing battle. The tyranny of being poor, the scruffiness of their acquaintance, the habits of discipline and order, all took their toll. The middle class reclaimed them. Within a year they were back in a small, well-organized apartment. Tom was working for a market research firm; Frady had been reinstated by the public school system. They were both clean-shaven.

But those two years on the outside had been the most exciting in Frady's life. Exciting not only because it had been his first, last and only attempt to escape the prison of his upbringing, but because during it he had discovered within himself a powerful steadfastness. He had been true—true to Tom. Through all their wanderings, all the strains of smalltown life and big city life, he had not once been diverted from his attachment. Although he knew Tom's faults, Frady never faltered. Tom was his and he was Tom's. Occasionally he wondered at the novelty of this—he had never been noted for his monogamy before—but there was no escape. "It must be chemical," he mused to himself sometimes. "Chemical" was the word for the mystery of his steadfastness.

It was Tom who had finally wanted out. His decision to leave had been conveyed as they both sat in the bleachers of a school playground near their home, watching some neighborhood kids play ball. "I have to get out," Tom had said in a strangled voice that Frady knew was the prelude to genuine tears. "I can't take it any more."

He was referring to their apartment just a few blocks away, now organized the way Frady liked. But Frady knew it wasn't just the apartment Tom wanted to escape, nor even himself. It was a whole net of responsibility, obligation, that had to be cast off. Sitting in the bleachers, watching the tears begin to wet Tom's face, Frady understood that his own steadfastness was Tom's foe. While he held fast, Tom struggled to get loose. The harder he clutched, the less air reached Tom. Now their lives had come apart. There was no cure for it.

He looked up at the facade of the house, as if it might offer some solace. Why couldn't he let go of Tom? It had been a good five years and their loving friendship had continued for the next fifteen. But now it was over. He didn't even know where on the face of the planet Tom might be at this moment. *Why didn't he let go?*

This time he saw it clearly. The curtain moving, the hand withdrawing. He sat very still, his heart hammering, wondering how long he'd been observed. For a moment he felt the urge to dash out. Then he stood up and made himself wait. It wouldn't be long.

The footsteps sounded very faintly at first, then louder. The tap-tap of heels on the tile staircase. For an instant, quite irrationally, he visualized the black shoes his grandmother wore. Then the door opened.

She was much older, but her back was still straight and her eyes still bright and black.

"*Ay, señor.*" She brought her ancient hands together in a spectral clap.

"Encarnación."

She stepped into the garden. Her face was lacy with wrinkles. He saw stars, flowers, snowflakes. He walked over and hugged her. She felt very frail in his arms and her skin smelled faintly of olive oil. He had the brief impression he was hugging time, or Spain, or the Old World.

"*Yo le ví arriba!*" Of course she'd seen him from upstairs. She often peered down at them as they sat in the garden, interrupting her housework, her dishwashing and bedmaking to check up on the tenants. She'd been attached to this house for fifty years. The real estate agent had told them what to pay her.

She was talking rapidly now and he barely understood. She hadn't recognized him at first. She thought he was a thief. Then she'd remembered. *El señor americano. Los dos señores americanos.*

She looked at him vaguely. She was trying to figure out which one he was. But it should have been easy. She had adored Tom. They'd hit it off instantly, communicating at some level he couldn't share, at a level where Tom's school Spanish didn't matter. Tom claimed she knew right off that he came from dirt farmers, poor Okies who'd worked a soil as exhausted as this. And she reminded him of his grandmother, a mean old biddy who sat with the hens all day and spat tobacco juice.

Now she'd placed him. He was not Tom. He was the other one. She smiled toothlessly. "*Y su amigo?*" Her voice changed from its reedy singsong, became warmer and more alert. Frady was swept by loss as he tried to explain that Tom had moved to California and after that to the Far East. But these names had no place in Encarnación's lexicon. She blinked and repeated her question. "Ca-li-for-nia." He gave it a Spanish pronunciation. Didn't everyone know about that golden state? But Encarnación did not. He was not Tom. Tom was not here. Suddenly she lost interest. She slouched. Frady had the impression that her straight back had been only a pose, a last bit of bravery, and that underneath her bones were badly bent.

And then, as if by magic, she straightened up again. She smiled and touched his arm. He summoned up his last intuitions and made sense of her Spanish. She wanted him to come home with her. To her house across the field. She had something to show him.

She moved closer. He caught the faint smell of olive oil again. Even as he resisted the idea of accompanying her, he knew he would accept. There was no way not to go. It was all part of this day's journey.

He waited while she took a huge key from her apron pocket and locked the front door, which was a bright blue. Then they crossed the garden to the back gate, the one reserved for her use. She lived across the field now planted with artichokes—a cash crop. He followed, noting how her heels imprinted the soft soil. He had never been invited to her house before. It was one of the smaller, poorer ones in this poor village.

As he expected, the sitting room was sparsely furnished—a cabinet, a few rush chairs, a scarred table. There were some mezzotints on the wall, a Sacred Heart over the fireplace. After he sat down she went to another room and returned with a bottle of Fundador and some olive-wood cups. She filled one and put it in front of him. Then she sat across from him, folded her hands and smiled. He wondered if this was what he had come for—to see her house.

After he had finished the Fundador and refused a second cup, she stood up and went to the cabinet in the corner. From it she took a large magazine, a rotogravure. It was an old issue of *Hoy*. He could see the Generalissimo on the cover, reviewing some Falangist troops. A disgusting sight. She opened the magazine to the centerfold.

She was babbling at him in Spanish that made no sense. He shook

his head, trying to stop her, unsuccessfully. And then she was present-
ing him with . . . what? He looked up. She was beaming. He shook his
head again.

"Murcia," she whispered.

He looked at the spread pages of the magazine again. Pressed flat, its
leaves black, its bloom the color of dried blood, was a dead rose. "*La
rosa de Murcia*," Encarnación whispered.

His skin prickled and he felt slightly sick. It was really an ugly sight, a
decayed bit of vegetation. But that wasn't it. Not at all.

He struggled with his recollections, seeking and avoiding, casting a
line into the past and resisting the catch, until at last it came up.

He and Tom had been touring mainland Spain. They'd finally
reached Murcia, which was Encarnación's birthplace. Tom was determined to find some souvenir to take back to her on Mallorca.

He'd spotted it while Frady was contemplating the facade of the
cathedral, stirred by the sight of moonlight on old stone. He had looked
around, about to repeat Goethe's phrase about baroque architecture
being frozen music, but there was no Tom. He saw only two *guardias
civiles*, their patent leather helmets reflecting the moonlight.

And then, unexpectedly, the *guardias* were running and shouting.
Frady knew they were running after Tom.

"Frady! Over here!" He looked to his left. Tom, grinning mischiev-
ously, was behind a fence. Frady could see rows and rows of plants —
small tea roses.

"Here!" Tom cupped a rosebush by its thorn-free bottom, yanked
and tossed it to Frady over the fence. Then he ran off. The *guardias*
chased after him.

Frady waited until they were on the other side of the plaza, then
picked up the stolen rosebush. He hid it behind his back until he found
some newspapers. Then he rolled it up.

By the time he got back to their hotel room he was furious. He had
actually abetted Tom in the theft, helped him get a thrill from some
petty and illegal escapade. The rosebush, now sitting on the dresser of
the hotel room, was the evidence. The only hitch was, Franco's police
weren't like the cops back home. For all he knew, they'd both get into
serious trouble.

He was about to take the incriminating rosebush downstairs and
dump it when the door opened. He wheeled around guiltily. It was
Tom. His face was alight with glee. He was, Frady could see, vastly

pleased with himself. Once the *guardias* had found out he was American they had given him a lecture about respecting the customs of the country. Then they had released him. They had actually driven him back to the hotel in one of their cars.

Frady found himself listening to all this with profound irritation. At last he said, "What the hell did you take it for?"

Tom's eyes widened. "For Encarnación! Who do you think?"

"For Encarnación!"

And then, as he watched Tom on the other bed, his face catlike with pleasure, Frady had started to laugh. At the stupidity, the childishness, the silliness of it. Of course Tom would do something like this. It was just his style—making waves, stirring things up, skirting disaster.

"If there's no trouble involved, the gift isn't worth anything. Whaddya think, I was gonna go in a souvenir shop and buy her a *bota?*"

Tom was on his feet now, inspecting the rosebush. He took it in the bathroom and dropped it into the bidet, which he filled with water. As Frady watched, it occurred to him that this little adventure was part of an old promise too—just as the nightingale had been. In his anger, his fear, his relief, he was as intensely alive as he would ever be.

Encarnación was still holding out the magazine with its hideous relic, still beaming. She didn't know anything about the theft, the *guardias*, the scene in the hotel room. For her it only mattered that the rosebush came from Murcia, her beloved Murcia. She had treasured the plant, and this, probably its last offspring, for twenty years.

And then Frady saw quite clearly that Tom had touched Encarnación's life with fire too. It had blazed up as brightly, as briefly, as his own. Tom had been an addiction for her too.

"*Llévela consigo.*" It was Encarnación. She wanted him to take the rose. To carry it off with him. He looked up. Her hand, outstretched, was fretted with tiny lines. Her face was beatific with love. And then, taking the rose, he understood what she had in mind. She wanted him to find Tom and return the rose.

"No!" he started to shout, feeling angry and betrayed at the same time, but suddenly it wasn't necessary. The movement of his hand had decapitated the rose. Its petals, hematic brown flakes, drifted to the floor. In his hand remained a bit of dry stalk. He heard her sharp intake of breath, then he dropped the stalk. It floated to a spot among the petals.

"That's the end of the rose of Murcia," he said quite loudly in

English. Then he put out his hand. She was observing him with large black eyes. He knew she had heard something in his voice, but whether it was the snapping of a chain or merely the harshness of his native tongue he did not know. At last she took his outstretched hand in both of hers. She was waiting for something more — an embrace perhaps — but he didn't make a move. It was the smell of olive oil that repelled him, but it was something else too. He turned, heading for the door. What else? As he opened the door a little breeze darted in and stirred up the brown flakes on the floor. With a goodbye nod he stepped out, closing the door behind him.

He set off toward the town plaza and the bus stop. Less than two hours had passed since he'd arrived; he might still catch the early afternoon bus back to Palma. What was it? he asked himself again, recalling a painting of the Roman soldier at Pompeii who had remained at his post even though Vesuvius had erupted and buried him in lava for twenty centuries.

It came to him as he boarded the bus and settled himself in a rear seat. She reeked of steadfastness. And then, as the bus started, it came to him that he had reached the very heart of his trouble. Faithfulness, a secular version of the love of God, had crippled him. Virtue had been transformed into vice. He had turned into that monster, the keeper of the flame. He shivered, though the bus was quite warm, and the absurd notion came to him that he would wither like the rose of Murcia unless he could forget everything that had ever happened to him in this village.

Alex was out of sorts, but Frady had expected it. He knew it from the curt greeting on his arrival in their hotel room, and a reluctance to look up from the book Alex held in his hand. It was the history of Mallorca. He'd gotten as far as the Inquisition.

After a few inquiries about the presents Alex had bought for his children — gifts now piled on the dresser — Frady went into the bathroom to shower. He wondered how much to tell Alex about the day, searching for the words that would make it clear.

They went to an early dinner, at a place in the old part of town. The restaurant, under an arcade, specialized in soufflés. It was called El Siglo. Frady had often come here with Tom — it had been their special place — but that information didn't seem worth imparting tonight. Instead, he watched Alex carefully, noting his familiar habits — how he took out half-moon glasses to read the menu, how he tapped his cigarette exactly four times before putting it in his mouth, how he broke his bread neatly in half, then in quarters, before buttering it. Alex chewed very slowly; he was a deliberate eater. Once it had taken him an hour to eat an artichoke.

And then Frady saw, with devastating clarity, what the rest of his life with Alex would be like. It would consist of slow meals and quiet nights and sex once a week. There would be no fear, no anger, but a great deal of sweetness and companionship and comfort. It would be rather like life in a nursing home.

Alex hadn't spoken much through the meal. He had, of course, sensed Frady's tension, his preoccupation. In his usual mild way he was waiting. Once or twice he searched Frady's face—causing Frady a twinge of remorse. It was really up to him to explain his day. It affected them both. But he wasn't ready for that—not yet.

After dinner they walked slowly down the Borne, toward the waterfront, absorbing the soft air, the sight and sound of the other strollers, the plink of a guitar coming from a café. It was their custom to walk their dinner down. Once or twice Alex put his hand to the small of Frady's back. It was a motion that had always struck him as sweetly tender—Alex wanting to shelter him or propel him, or merely touch him. But tonight, in his unsettled state, Alex's touch struck him as the dead hand of the future. He could read the rest of his life in that slight pressure.

And then, quite unexpectedly, he knew what he had to do. It came to him in a blaze of color—the color, in fact, of one of the roses planted in the center of the promenade on which they were now strolling. He felt quite dizzy as the plan took possession of him and for a moment he thought he couldn't do it. It was too difficult, too out of character. But the next moment he knew he had no choice. If his life was going to blaze again, if it was going to be filled with the sound of nightingales, it was up to him to arrange it. There was no one else around to do the job.

Without looking left or right he stepped into the planted area and yanked up a purple rosebush by its roots. When he straightened up, he and Alex were the center of a small circle of people.

"What are you doing?" It was Alex, whispering.

Brushing at the dirt, he held out the rosebush. "It's a souvenir." Alex put his hands behind his back and stepped away. He looked mortified.

Frady started to laugh. In the next instant he was aware of a refreshing and lustful joy rising in his veins.

"Put that back," Alex hissed, coming forward. But Frady continued laughing. He knew exactly how Alex felt.

And then, as the circle of onlookers parted, a municipal officer dressed in blue stepped toward him. Frady turned, the pilfered rose held proudly, triumphantly aloft. It was not, he thought in a final moment of clarity, the rose of Murcia—that one was dissolved forever. This one was for today, and tomorrow.

A last burst of laughter escaped him. "Arrest me," he said to the guard, "I'm a thief."

The Lesson of the Master

My sponsor believes I should put it all down on paper. She proposed this with a pixie smile on her round face, after a meeting at which I spoke. Spoke of myself to three dozen kind but damaged faces, ex-alcoholics all, in a church basement not far from here. "Now you've done the hard part, this should be easy." I'm not sure she's right, but she is irresistible as usual. Not only because I like her but because she knows the appeal of words on a page to a scholar. Nothing is true until you set it down. The linguistic fallacy. That was my undoing in the first place, of course, leading me to the sixth floor at Misericordia.

Another bit of wisdom from my sponsor comes to mind. "You can only be honest for yourself, you can't be honest for anyone else." Perhaps she was thinking of Toby, who was so much a part of my story. But I'm getting ahead of myself—I don't really think Toby ever had the least inkling of what truth meant. For him it was an alien concept, shot through with American Puritanism.

So I have bought this blue notebook. I write in it for an hour each morning. It will help me decide on my future. It may even reveal some last bit of self-deception. Or—a final irony—it may be only the most subtle trick of all, a trick played with words and mirrors and the illusion of understanding.

If I start at the beginning, I will have to show you the half-timbered house on the edge of Albany where I lived with two strangers, my mother and father. It was cold country outside, bleak and windswept nine months of the year, but even colder inside. My father worked as a construction supervisor for the state government, building cement bunkers for clerks—a job that eventually made him as smooth and featureless as the facades he erected. My mother, a tireless, grasping woman, originally from Tennessee, dreamed of being an intimate friend of the Governor's wife. She never succeeded.

By the time I reached adolescence, we just tolerated each others' presences in the house. You could probably spin some fashionable psychological theory from this, but I won't. I would rather point out that some people have a gift for childhood and others do not. I don't really think my parents were to blame for my boredom and disinterest; it was just a case of mismatched needs. They wanted a little carbon copy of themselves while I wanted out of the ignominy of youth as soon as possible.

Yet I owe to my parents, whom I now keep enshrined in photos around the apartment, the most significant event of my life.

The volume, in its binding of supple green morocco with the title stamped in gold, had been bought at a garage sale somewhere and never read. Just squashed on a shelf between two travel books, waiting: *The Great Short Novels of James Anthony Dedward.* Even now, after so much, the name rolls around on my tongue like an organ tone and I can, with a little effort, relive that moment when I lay on the couch in the sun parlor—a couch with a slippery taffeta cover of black and ivory stripes—and opened the book for the first time, noting its twin columns of dense type, its flimsy paper, its ornate chapter headings. How, you might ask, could a book like this attract a boy who'd never read anything but Robin Hood and King Arthur and Huck Finn, a boy whose extremities tingled every night with the sheer malevolence of adolescence? I don't know—not now, not then. I can only say that when I started to read, my teenage anguish was forgotten, the shouts of the baseball players across the street were unheeded, the noises of vacuum cleaner and garbage trucks unheard. I was swept up in those complex tales set in times and places far from Albany but instantly recognizable as my true home. How to describe here, in this sad apartment where I've started to pick up the threads of my life, my heart-swelling attraction to these stories of American naïfs and philandering Europeans and hypocritical aristocrats, all wandering the world almost a century before? How to explain my instant attraction to *Princess Tomassina, An International Scandal, The Spurious Zoffany?*

My mother certainly wasn't happy with my new enthusiasm. "You'll ruin your eyes on that small type," she said, the first time she came home from an afternoon selling suburban real estate, to find me on the taffeta couch in the darkening room, steeped in the sinister ambiance of the Hôtel des Trois Empereurs where young Croydon had just been abandoned by the heartless Amelia Glose. When I didn't answer, she said, more harshly, "Those stories are too old for you." I didn't bother to explain.

One afternoon, after selling a semidetached to a couple from Toronto, my mother came home from the local library with an armload of Penrod books. I looked at them to be polite, but I knew right away they weren't for me. What could highjinks in Indiana and pranks on the banks of the Wabash give me that Venice and Ferney and the Château de Chillon could not? How could the misdeeds of that tiresome Hoosier, who would probably stay a joker all his life, compare with the hinged sentences, the splendid irony, the fearful algebra of greed and folly and ambition laid out by James Anthony Dedward, the only American who interested me?

My mother returned the books before the due dates.

Frankly, I was unpleasantly precocious. A monster. When company came for dinner and asked me questions, I would first request that they address me as Michael, not Sonny. I hated my nickname, intended to distinguish me from my father, also Michael. After that, when they'd ask me friendly questions about school and sports, I'd answer in long involuted sentences full of words I had just read. The visitors would sit transfixed while a look of horror dawned on their faces and my parents laughed with embarrassment. I was rarely asked more than two questions. Yes, a monster. After I'd been too smart, I became horribly aware that my behind stuck out. A monster and deformed too. About this time my father started threatening to send me to military school. It would make a man out of me. Luckily, they couldn't afford it.

My reading habits isolated me from my contemporaries too. How could it have been otherwise? While they were talking about football and basketball and swapping bubble-gum cards, I was rehearsing in my mind whether Mademoiselle de Courcy had been right to go unchaperoned to the Colosseum on a night of full moon and whether Raeburn Tippett had made a fatal misstep when he invited Hyacinth DeMar to spend the holidays with him. How could my classmates possibly understand the deep, almost choking, pleasure that I derived from those burnished tales? Mentioning them was a risk not to be run.

Some of the girls in my class tried to make friends, but I had nothing to do with them, knowing I'd be even more of an outcast if my only companions were girls.

Of course, I'd dream of friendship in those days—or rather of a Friend. A Friend was not a common noun but a title, like King or President or Czar. I suppose this was natural, considering the long hours I lay sprawled on the taffeta couch. There had to be some balance, some way to reenter boyhood from the strange angle at which I lived it.

Finally, when I was fourteen, I found him. His name was Bud Gorman. He had blue eyes, a bony face with freckles, a taut boy-man torso. Our relationship reached its apex when we broke into vacant houses together—he leading the way, I following. I was breathless with hero worship. But under that, I see now, was something more refined—the desire to cut through the scruples, the obligations, that enclosed me. Afterwards, warmed by the outlawry of our explorations, we would go to our cave hideout, where I would feed him summaries of the stories I'd been reading. I always wanted him to hold me, to cradle me in those stringy arms with budding muscles, but aside from a casual brush in the course of our adventures, I never came within a foot of him.

After Bud's family moved to Oregon, I looked for a replacement without success. His face—all flat planes and sharp angles—became the one I looked for. Many years later I realized there is only one face you love in a lifetime. You may see many faces but the one you love remains, the single visage behind the many. Bud's face, *mutatis mutandis*, has accompanied me for thirty years.

I chose to go to Medford University in New York because Byron Wick taught there. Wick was Dedward's great biographer. When the fifth and final volume of the *Life* appeared, he won every literary prize around.

When I first encountered him I saw a short white-haired man, flecked with tobacco and given to flowered waistcoats. This was some months after my arrival. It had taken me that long to get up the courage to visit him. I remember I got ready for the appointment with nervous care, choosing a green velvet jacket that seemed faintly Victorian and a printed foulard (yellow and brown) sticking from the pocket. I planned to refer to my outfit as inspired by that of Jack Longstraw in *The Altar of Art*.

Well, undergraduates are like that still—at least some of them. But I was wasting my time with Byron Wick. He wasn't interested in dithering about Dedward. When I mentioned the green volume with the supple leather binding and the taffeta couch of my childhood, he stopped my gushing. "Dedward has that effect on some youngsters, what can I do for you?"

When I told him I wanted to make Dedward the subject of my honors thesis, he tried to discourage me. "That's been pretty well mined out, have you got any new ideas?" Of course, at that age I didn't and he terminated the interview abruptly. I went back to the dormitory quite depressed, my inheritance suddenly snatched away. Now I know what that inheritance is worth but then, nineteen years old, the solo years in Albany a weight on my heart, I wondered if I could survive without the dream of Dedward. Where did I belong if not in that magical corpus, a body of work which I had now read twice from beginning to end while making copious notes?

I certainly didn't belong in the dorm, a few blocks from the campus buildings and filled with raucous lechers of both sexes, who seemed only a slight improvement on the sports-happy clods of Benjamin Franklin High. I certainly didn't feel at home in New York, billed in the Medford catalog as "a prime resource for students," but which reduced me to a faceless, nameless cipher. In fact, solitude had already begun to claim me, the beastly solitude which Dedward had warned against, and which, though I didn't yet know it, constituted the deepest, most infrangible, link between us. That solitude, almost prenatal in its intensity, returned after my talk with Wick and I wallowed in it with a kind of voluptuous misery. It is only now, after going through the pain at its center, that I have been able to reach the other side.

I don't remember the exact moment when Byron Wick began to take me seriously. It was at the end of my sophomore year and might have been thanks to Louisa Rosenquist, who liked some of the papers I wrote for her course on literary criticism. Or it might have been because I always signed up for Wick's courses and laughed at his genteel Edwardian jokes. Or it might have been something more sinister altogether—the fact that I reeked of fatal aestheticism. He might have seen in me the young prig my classmates did, dead in the center but surrounded by an awful hunger. If so, he must have been reassured because one day after class I heard myself being invited for a drink.

Maybe my later excesses began with that first drink at the Medford Faculty Club, under the shrewd gaze of the founding merchants. Wick suggested, over a second round, that I proof the galleys of his new book. He looked at me quite dryly and added, "It's not about Dedward, so don't get excited."

Actually, it was the journal of a Dedward contemporary, a minor American novelist but great magazine editor, who didn't exactly fascinate me. Still, it was an honor. It would mean working with Wick, visiting him at home. I suppose I looked as if I'd just been struck by lightning, because Wick patted me on the arm and told me to take it easy, I had my whole life ahead of me. That pat, believe it or not, seemed an initiation of sorts, an introduction to the holy rituals ahead. Oh, the absurdities of literary undergraduates.

After we parted, I was too excited and, let's face it, too high to go home. I decided to celebrate by going to a nearby bar, a place on Eighth Street called Jenny's. I'd walked past it many times but had never ventured in.

I can still summon up the fear and defiance that accompanied me as I stepped through the door. It seemed I was entering an underworld or antiworld, where nothing I had ever done before counted. I believe that, deep down, I expected to run into Bud Gorman.

I ordered a Manhattan—the only kind of cocktail I'd tried in those days—and looked around cautiously. I saw men of all sorts, mostly blank-faced and unapproachable. Many were wearing business suits. Suddenly it struck me that they were all grown-up versions of Huck Finn and Penrod. Not one of them could compare with the shades and shadows of my mind, with the hellishly-lit heroes of literature. You see, the fatal dream was already at work, the dream that would eventually lead me to the sixth floor at Misericordia.

Despite this, I found myself drifting toward a man my own age sitting at the end of the bar. His face, studded with tiny bristles, seemed to promise something. I thought, after my second or third drink, that a man with a face like that had marched with Caesar or fought in the marshes of Dacia. But I was wrong. His name was Jerry and he was in the insurance business. He hoped to win big in the New York State lottery. A little later, I put down my drink and walked out. Solitude was better than boredom.

By the time I reached my senior year, certain patterns had been set. I was Byron Wick's pet. Not the heir apparent—not yet, anyway—but privy to his thoughts, fears, spites. I shared with him a horror over certain Marxist reinterpretations of the later works; over the appropriation of Dedward by the structuralists, who saw in his hermetic life and ornate texts the biographical disjunction they sought; over the feminist endorsement of the American novels with their strong-minded heroines; over the reductionist readings of certain relationships by the radical homosexuals.

Yes, I was his pet, the echo and mirror of his mind. On how many afternoons did I haunt the booksellers on Fourth Avenue, the Berg Collection, the yellow ledgers at Harper's, all at Professor Wick's direction? On how many evenings did we sit in the study of his apartment while his wife glided in and out, petit point in hand, to refill our brandy glasses? It was a splendid situation for a young man from the provinces.

I wasn't always able to ignore the demands of my flesh, of course. I was young, New York was a giant playpen, and there was liquor to help it along. My repertory had now expanded from manhattans to martinis, margaritas and stingers. But you mustn't think I drank out of despair in those days. No. I wanted a cocktail when my elation was unmanageable, when I saw the world as so beautiful, so graspable, that my breath came short and my knees trembled. Alcohol was a fixative: it caught my vision and sealed it in a chamber where I might turn it over and over like a crystal paperweight.

Still, there were signs if I'd cared to look. After five or six drinks, I'd find somebody and make a slurred proposition. We couldn't go back to the dorm but there were other places — places where five minutes was long enough. I never took my clothes off. It seemed impossible to relinquish that much of myself. Afterwards I dismissed the whole thing as a fantasy.

Yes, by the time I graduated from Medford, the pattern had been set. There was my work — and my life. I was caught in a dichotomy familiar enough to psychiatrists, but with the solipsism of youth I fancied myself the first, not the last, in a long line.

I spent the summer after graduation in England, carrying letters from Professor Wick to various librarians, archivists, collectors, who were probably amused by my American eagerness, but were kind enough not to show it. I also visited some of Dedward's haunts, traveling down to Bath, retracing his walks through London, visiting his grave. At certain times, as I walked through Green Park or stood before the Royal Crescent, I was filled with the notion that he had just departed, that he might still appear — dressed in his frock coat, amber-headed cane in hand, ready for his constitutional. When I told Professor Wick this, he told me it was an occupational affliction of biographers and to beware.

I will pass over my graduate years since they were a repeat of the previous four. I worked as a teaching assistant, selected a subject for my dissertation and continued my weekend forays to the bars. Only two events of these years are worth mentioning — I got my own apartment, near Professor Wick's, and attended the retirement dinner given him by the university. By that time they had created the James Anthony Dedward Chair of Literature for him. Now, at 65, he had to relinquish it to a Trinity man named O'Reilly who, to my mind, had no real credentials and had gotten the post through the ceaseless application of macushla charm. The dinner was one of those sad but thrilling affairs that mark a watershed. The university deans, pinching pennies as usual, served chicken à la king but redeemed themselves by placing before each of us for dessert a *bombe glacée* with a crack running down one side. Byron Wick's speech has been widely reprinted, so I won't quote it here. It was the final testament of a life spent in service to a quest. He spoke of the religion of art, the salvation of the word, as if the atomic bomb had never been invented. As I listened, I thought that we were a pair, Byron Wick and I, even though separated by forty years.

As a young Ph.D., dissertation in hand (*Dedward in Italy, 1879-1886*), I had only a few choices for a job: Anniston, Alabama; Potsdam, New York; an engineering school near Denver. Alabama I dismissed out of Yankee chauvinism and Potsdam was too near Albany and my parents. That left Colorado. I drove out in a new Rabbit, my books piled high in the back, feeling as if I were headed into exile. What, I wondered, would I find in the West?

Well, let me say that I was used to solitude, but nothing like this. The Rockies looked down with malign indifference. The other faculty members found me a little specialized for their tastes, which ran to camping, skiing and having babies. The students were better — sweet, with spacious and unspoiled minds — but not much in the way of afterhours companionship. I bought a bulldog, whom I christened Harriet, and spent my evenings reading.

Weekends were the worst. I couldn't go to the bars and baths in

Denver for fear of running into my students. Sometimes I'd call an escort service but mostly I cruised in my car.

Denver is full of handsome robots down on their luck. I found them at bus-stops mostly, tall young men with clear skin and a fierce emptiness in their eyes. The smell of burnt-out synapses could bring you to your knees. They accepted my offer of a drink and hopped into the Rabbit with no compunction about the eventual price. They were invariably affectionate toward Harriet, who would go mad with the attention. When we'd blotted up as much as we could hold, we'd rub against each other under the blankets and fall asleep. In the morning we were full of lies. It wasn't much but it kept me from going crazy. By the end of three or four years I was avoided by most of my colleagues. Sometimes when I was alone and badly hung over, I'd recall what Dedward had called Oscar Wilde: unclean beast.

Still, life went on. I was plugged into the worldwide Dedward network and eventually became secretary of the Dedward Society. I made flying trips to seminars and conferences; I spent a sabbatical year in Europe. Professor Wick, whom I now addressed by his first name, stopped enroute to his retirement home in California, dispensing encouragement. He was active in my behalf. He hoped to get me back to Medford, my alma mater. With a little luck and pressure in the right places . . .

Now, when the results are in, I can see it might have been better if I'd stayed in the mountains with my handsome humanoids. The division between my two worlds would have remained complete. And I would never have heard of Florence Pallant Coombs or Toby Bellosguardo. But, during my seventh year in Colorado, the appointment to Medford came through. I was almost forty years old and in most important ways had not progressed beyond the man-child who had dreamed his afternoons away on a striped taffeta couch in Albany.

I gave Harriet to my neighbors, who adored her, and after one last kiss on her beautiful-ugly face, packed up the Rabbit with my expanded possessions and retraced my route to the East. As the towers of Manhattan came into view, gleaming in the westerly sun, I thought they were merely a new, more advanced version of the coppery buttes I had viewed in Colorado. As usual, I was distorting things.

Now, I can only wonder at the fate that brought me Florence Pallant Coombs and Toby Bellosguardo at almost the same time—

the first so long dead, the second so disturbingly alive. It was like a one-two punch, or one of those pincers movements in tank warfare. They were not connected, though — at least not at first. How could they be? Pallant Coombs lay under a rectangle of Roman earth, in the Protestant cemetery near the pagan pyramid that Piranesi drew; Toby was in my office, my classes, my home. I will tell you about the dead one first because it's easier.

It was the merest chance that I came across the notice. It was one of those accidents that change lives. It occurred toward the end of my first year back at Medford, a time of false, early spring. A bookseller on 58th Street had mailed me an auction notice and a catalog. The entry read, "Miscellaneous Papers of Florence Pallant Coombs, 1838-1894." The lot number was 541. She was described as an author. That was my period and the name was vaguely familiar. I looked her up. She was one of a breed of cross-Atlantic lady writers, footnoted occasionally nowadays, but essentially unreadable. Prolific and senti-mental, she'd turned out almost two dozen novels, specializing in loyal daughters whose love was betrayed by a succession of black-guards, dastards, brigands, etc. Her big bestseller was *Audrey*.

Noting all this, I could feel something nibbling at the edges of my memory, something quite fresh and urgent, tinged with mystery rather than banality. What could it be? I took a long stroll through the Village after leaving the library, trying to get a fix on it. There had been many three-named American ladies in the last century who wrote forgettable books, but this one seemed different.

It came to me over a postprandial brandy in my living room, over-looking a Japanese cherry tree on Tenth Street which had bloomed too soon and too ardently and, not unlike the heroines of Ms. Coombs, been clobbered by a change in the weather. Sipping my brandy, I saw the volume quite clearly. It was an inexpensive reprint from the middle period, containing some of his more popular tales. The in-scription sizzled in the air, the large, disordered scrawl as familiar as my own: "To my great and good friend, F.P.C., with immutable affection." Under it, of course, his own full name.

The three initials crawled up the wall of my mind as I fitted them to the catalog notice the way you'd fit the head of an Artemis to a torso. I remember standing up with a yelp, my head miraculously clear of the wine, and shouting, "Of course, of course."

I had seen the book in the reconstituted library in the house at

Bath, the shelves filled again with as many of Dedward's books as could be pried loose from admirers, collectors, booksellers. Byron Wick, I realized with guilty triumph, had not seen that restored library, nor the inscribed copy. It came too late to be included in his biography. At this moment I was the only person in the world who could connect James Anthony Dedward and Frances Pallant Coombs.

I had a chance to examine lot 541 in a small room above the main floor of the Argosy, the dealer watching me carefully as I riffled through the papers. I handled poems, watercolors, a journal, dress-maker receipts, letters to and from Memphis and—more to the point—a dozen letters in Dedward's loose hand, all dating from the last years of his correspondent's life. "Fairly interesting," I remarked to Mr. Conrad, who tugged at a nicotine-stained mustache while, no doubt, calculating his future profits. "I might bid on them if no one else does." He was too smart for that—nonchalance is probably what he hopes for in a prospect—and smiled sagely. "There has been a lot of interest in that box already," he said.

The auction took place a week later. I might have gotten backing from the university or one of the private libraries, but something told me not to share my find. I'd invest all my savings if I had to.

Bad luck dogged me. After a few bidders dropped away I found my-self locked in combat with a tall woman in pants, a grey mink slung over her shoulders. Later I found she was the patroness of a feminist press on Long Island. The room went still with delight as she kept raising me by hundreds, until we reached three thousand. Then, after whispering to an unkempt woman at her side, she desisted. After-wards she came up to me and remarked without apology that she'd gotten confused. She'd really come to bid on the documents of one Florence Combs, a Chicago suffragette born fifty years later.

I put the ragged contents of lot 541 in my attaché case after writing the check. Mr. Conrad's face was a study in satisfaction. "A very great writer," he said smugly, but of course he knew nothing about her.

I knew I should xerox the dozen Dedward letters and mail them to Byron Wick, now living in Monterey, but I didn't. Call it greed, hog-gishness, the hope of glory—whatever you like. But I sincerely be-lieved it concerned only Dedward, Pallant Coombs and myself.

Oh yes. One other person. Toby Bellosguardo. I suppose I can post-pone that part of my story no longer.

He chose me as his doctoral adviser with unerring instinct. I remember the occasion, because it was two days after I had acquired the Pallant Coombs material. I was in my office, mulling over my first, quite superficial, study of the letters, when the door to my office opened without a knock and a tall young man appeared. He was dressed in boutique style, international division—a safari jacket, short-sleeved, over a linen shirt by Ruccelli, lizard belt, suede pants, bicycle shoes. He wasn't in the least apologetic about barging in. Later I would find out he never apologized for anything. In a low voice, with an accent I couldn't yet place, he said he'd been trying to find me for several days. He smiled, his bony, angular face elongating, and at the same time managed to look accusing. It was a combination of courtesy and arrogance I didn't often find in my students, whose aim was mostly to placate me. "Who are you?" I asked.

After he identified himself, he remarked that he found the other teachers "uninteresting," and had decided to try me. He announced this as if he were doing me a favor. Then he took a cigarette from his safari shirt, clicked an expensive lighter, and blew smoke at me.

I was just beginning to get huffy when he began to speak in a grave monotone. I confess the accent intrigued me—it's a game I've always enjoyed. Italian, I thought first, after hearing his name, then amended it to Hungarian, followed by south German. He had trouble with the *th* sound—exploding it into little dentals, and with his *r*'s, which turned glottal. On the other hand, there was no unnecessary stretch of the vowels. I had just decided on Greek with a Swiss education when he told me he had been born in Istanbul to a consular family—a father from Parma, a mother from Utrecht—and had lived in Italian legations and embassies for most of his childhood. He told me this with an easy self-absorption, never raising his voice, never seeking my approval or measuring my reaction. I had the impression that he was simply including me in the charmed circle of his life. He might have been dispensing a benediction.

When he finished he looked at me with serious raccoon eyes—both deep and glassy—and waited. For the first time in many years I found myself uneasy in the presence of a student. I had the brief notion that I was losing control of the situation, that a white light was illuminating a landscape I had long forgotten, and that I would do better to refuse his request for an adviser. At the same time, in that corner of my mind where no lies are possible, I knew I would accept. As we talked about courses and dissertation subjects and New York, I had to be careful not to look at him too hard—at the angles and planes of his face, at his square hands and spatulate fingers, at the sprinkling of hair like golden grass which filled the vee of his collar. For one terrifying moment, as he leaned over to stub out his cigarette, I imagined the rest of him under the clothes and I had the sudden impression that he was Bud Gorman come back to destroy me. Fortunately, that moment passed. I told him I would give him my decision in a week. His undergraduate work, in a bevy of European and midwestern American schools, did not sound reassuring. I would have to look up his record. There were other considerations.

He turned at the door just before leaving and said, "I was right, you are interesting." Then he gave his accusing smile and walked on. By that time I had a name for him: the Orphan Prince.

Our second meeting took place a week later. This time he had gone American, turning up in tanktop and jeans, a knapsack balanced on one powerful shoulder. I thought of the sculptures of the Italian Renaissance, heavy bones moving under marble, osteal fragments subtending the skin. He seemed perfectly joined together, silver flesh dusted with golden hair, his face a masterpiece of lucid self-knowledge. You see, I was already preparing my own grave.

As before, he was casually condescending and utterly charming. He gave me his opinions unasked. Most of the teachers were either charlatans or senile. The only decent restaurants in the neighborhood had poorly stocked cellars. His preferred game was football, but he could only play it in Central Park on weekends with a group of Italian and Polish waiters, because Americans didn't appreciate the game. What we called football was a form of wrestling. Would I care to join him for dinner next week?—a filmmaker friend from Colombia was in town. I might find him "interesting."

I don't remember when I first realized he was flirting with me. Perhaps it was at that second meeting, or at the dinner with his Colombian friend. But it was done so discreetly, so casually, with what, for want of a better word, I would call humor, that at first I hardly noticed. I should have. Toby was like a fortune hunter in an early Dedward novel. Only he didn't collect American heiresses. He collected susceptible college professors, who were even more useful.

He wasn't a serious student. I found that out very quickly, when I suggested he use his extraordinary linguistic background to collate some recent Dedward translations with the originals. He gave me a sloppy report, unfit for publication, and when I criticized it—we were in the basement of the library—he got up and walked out. I watched him go with a stab of guilt. Had I been too harsh? Had I lost his esteem, his approval? I mention these things to show how quickly our roles had reversed themselves. By then I'd known him only a month but in many ways, in most important ways, I was his student.

It's important that I write down the truth. That's what this blue notebook is for. Toby got the upper hand very quickly. Maybe I was ready for him. Maybe the void at the center of my life had gaped too long. Maybe there were other needs, going back to my beginnings, which I was too foolish to acknowledge. I only know that he began to fill my thoughts, my plans, my privacies. In the evening, reading or watching TV, drink in hand, I would imagine that he was alongside, the empty air shaped to his form. Other times, when we were together, I'd listen to him for long stretches without interrupting. His life could not have been more different from mine.

I remember one story that may stand for the rest. In Sicily he'd made friends with an old family, once grandees of Palermo but now fallen on hard times. The Foscari clan still had a few valuable things, among them a gilt cross set with gems. They wanted him to take the cross to America and sell it—illegal under the Italian law safeguarding antiquities. With his diplomatic connections, his luggage wouldn't be searched. He would keep a commission of ten percent. They trusted him.

A look of casual contempt crossed his face as he told me, in imperfect English, what had happened. "When I arrive to New York, the art people, the big companies, do not much appreciate the Foscari cross. They look at it, they call in the experts, the Quattrocento students, they take a small piece of paint to see under microscope, and then they telephone me and say, this cross is made maybe last year, maybe ten years ago. I tell them no, not true, but they say, come get the cross, we don't want it." His look of contempt ripened into a sneer. "Foscari family is one of the famous in Sicily, in Italy. But you know, the art company is right. The cross not good. They cheat me. Junk." Toby let out a bark of laughter. Yes, those Sicilians had been cheating visitors for two thousand years; he was merely the latest. And then he had his bright idea.

"I went to the ambassador in Washington—he is the old friend of my father—and show him the cross. I tell him everything what happened except I want to sell the cross. I say, look, the Foscaris are giving away beautiful treasures that belong to the Italian people. I want to return it. To a museum in Naples, Rome, because I feel too bad."

There had been a scandal. The Foscaris had been fined for smuggling out antiquities despite their admission that the cross was a fake. The cross was now hanging in the Sacristy of San Giovanni in Rome.

The story, ugly as it was, filled me with delight, as did Toby's glee at his revenge. I thought again of the title I had bestowed on him: the Orphan Prince. He seemed to have escaped the afflictions of his American contemporaries. As he sat across an oak table from me in Cory's, a student hangout on Mercer Street, a Tiffany lamp staining us lime-green and blue, I saw in him the antidote to my own life. It didn't occur to me that I was simply fooling myself.

Sometimes Toby's friends joined us at Cory's. He was very easy with them. Young women especially fell under his spell. There was one, Karen Tyler, who used to come to our table and stand behind him, massaging his shoulders and back, strumming her thighs against him, while she talked about her classes. Sometimes he went off to sit with her. When he did, the others would watch me carefully. I suppose they knew before I did.

Certainly Luisa Rosenquist knew. She bustled into my office one day for a chat. She'd aged during my Denver years, her face more deeply lined, her hair lacquered into a Bernini canopy, more relentlessly black. But her warnings about socializing too much with students fell on deaf ears. I suppose the department was full of gossip about me. Even a place like Medford, in a city like New York, was basically a small town. But I wasn't sleeping with Tony Bellosguardo. I had never held that heavy body in my arms. I had merely thought about it during long evenings, punctuated by booze and solitary vice.

Oh, he came to visit me more than once. He would stalk through my rooms, examining the pictures, the books, the mementoes, as if he might inherit them some day. I would tag along, fighting the notion that he belonged here more than I did, turning aside his queries with a joke. But my heart would be beating rapidly and my voice would curl around us like a disembodied embrace.

Several times he sat beside me on the couch, moving with his drink from the chair where I had placed him. At these times I had to contend with two urges—to touch him and to run outside. He knew what I was going through, because his eyes would play over me and I could almost hear him purr.

Now, writing in this notebook, I try to understand what held me back—why I didn't just lead Toby into the bedroom, grab him and make him strip off his clothes. He would have been more than cooperative. It was what he expected—he and everyone else, in an age when couples were making beelines for bedrooms from coast to coast. But I didn't. I couldn't. Perhaps I was still lost in the labyrinth of my imagination, unable to let daylight into my life. Perhaps I was afraid it would be less than perfect. Perhaps I was simply afraid. But in some deep, instinctive part of me, I knew that the bed on which you clasp the creature of your dreams is really a deathbed.

By his fourth or fifth visit it was clear to both of us that nothing was going to happen. Nothing. I knew he knew this when he turned to me—we were side by side on the couch—and his smile, his mask of lightness, disappeared and I read contempt in his eyes. He had acquiesced in my refusal at last. Suddenly, strangely, I was reminded of the visitors to my parents' home in Albany who had asked me about school, expecting simple, friendly answers and had gotten evasion, trickery, literature.

When Toby got up to go, a few minutes later, I felt my exile from the natural order of things more deeply than ever before. I knew a terrible depression was waiting in the wings—a depression that had, perhaps, been waiting all my life.

When he left, I took out a row of bottles, untouched, and stood them on the coffee table. It was clear to me, though I didn't dare say it, that I wouldn't leave the house until I'd gone through them all.

I missed my classes for a week—and barely missed a few weeks at Smithers' too. Louisa threatened me with the detoxification center after she bullied my building superintendent into unlocking my door. But instead, in an act of charity I didn't know she was capable of, she bundled me into a taxi and over to her house, in the mews behind Fifth Avenue, where I convalesced in the sunshine filtering through a handsome plane tree just outside her window. Now I know she understood me perfectly—*perfectly*—but then I was under the delusion that my secret was mine alone.

After I recovered—thinner, paler, but steady—I didn't see Toby for a while. At Cory's they told me he'd gone to Washington, to stay at one of the embassies. In my disordered state I wondered if he was punishing me, then dismissed the idea. He was only doing what he always did—creating a world that served and indulged him.

In the meantime, there were the Dedward-Pallant Coombs papers. I had neglected them, as I had neglected myself, since meeting Toby Bellosguardo.

I took up my investigations again, fitting the clues in the letters and miscellaneous papers into other facts, other archives, that shimmered like a huge invisible web over the Master's life. It was a great relief to be back in that airy construction, where I knew my way around.

Armed with a letter of introduction to Dedward in London, Pallant Coombs had crossed the Atlantic, intending to stay a year or two. He was distant at first, patronizing. She was second-rate; he was, after all, Dedward. But little by little he thawed. They became slightly more than acquaintances. He showed her the sights, introduced her in certain drawing rooms. She was grateful. He became increasingly benign. He began to enjoy their talks. She treasured them, referring to him, in a letter to her sister in Memphis as "America's greatest resource."

But she decides, for reasons unknown, to leave London after a season and spend the rest of the year in Oxford. Perhaps she is researching a novel—this is not yet clear to me—or perhaps she is in some inner turmoil that requires her departure. Dedward writes to Oxford that he misses her, that London is "an inner sepulchre" without her. He goes up to Oxford to visit. His later journals, after the tragedy, refer to that "silver time" when they walked the cobbled lanes to the sound of churchbells. He sounds the themes he will tease into an amplitude in his last books—regret, missed opportunity, forbidden love.

And then—what? A crisis. I get hints only, from cryptic entries in her journal, from another letter to her sister in which she speaks of tears shed at night, of solitude, of a sudden decision to quit Oxford. A month later she is writing in her spidery hand from Venice, where she has taken lodging in a *quartiere mobigliato* with a view of the Salute. There is no record of any communication with Dedward, who has declined to a set of initials in her journal. Two months later, in a bout of delirium brought on by influenza, she leaps to her death through the window of her bedroom. She is found, a soft, crumpled heap, by a pair of midnight strollers.

Dedward, I learn from the sister's letters, rushes to Venice for the funeral. A niece has come down from Paris and from her Dedward manages to get back some but not all of his letters to Pallant Coombs, letters tied with a lavender ribbon. But of course he doesn't know of—or can't obtain—the journal in its red leather binding, tucked away in her trunk, and now in my possession.

And there you—or rather *I*—had it all. There was no clear statement as to the nature of the relationship between Dedward and Pallant Coombs. Even in her journal, the lady is discreet. The Victorians kept the doors to their bedrooms shut. The interpretation is left to me, my responsibility alone.

I don't know how word leaked out to the little world of Dedwardian scholarship. Perhaps Mr. Conrad at the Argosy had been boasting; perhaps, in my ravings at Louisa's I had let something slip. Perhaps it was just one of those discoveries that is suddenly in the air—emanations, auras—because the time is ripe. But I started to hear hints, receive queries through the mail, become the object of jokes about "spilling the beans on Dedward and his lady-friend." It was clear that something new, something revelatory, was expected. I put off the curious, of course, knowing my reputation was at stake. My conclusions would have to be perfectly defended, solid as a rock.

But that wasn't the real reason I postponed, equivocated, sat for long hours in my wing chair as the spring changed into summer and the school-term ended and Pallant Coombs' little diary with its violet-colored ink and its occasional drawings of anemones (her favorite flower) remained on my lap. No, there were other reasons—reasons going farther back and farther forward. From Toby to Bud Gorman, from this comfortable apartment to the striped taffeta couch of my childhood. Several times I thought of going to Louisa with the whole thing, admitting my confusion, dumping it in her lap. But I didn't. I suspect that I was enjoying the dilemma too much to end it, that I wanted to extract from it the only ingredient that would satisfy me— disaster. And so I talked it over with Toby.

I hadn't seen him, except at a distance, for almost two months. He hadn't come to my office, hadn't appeared at Cory's. Once or twice we passed in the hallways and stopped to exchange pleasantries. His face was tanned from tennis weekends in the Hamptons, his manner as carelessly arrogant as ever. I wondered if he was angling to change advisers—he would have arranged it without a qualm, I knew—but I was afraid to ask. When I invited him to dinner I had the unpleasant feeling that I was acting the rejected suitor, pleading for crumbs. But I wasn't, of course. It was I who had done the rejecting.

We had dinner in the Faculty Club, under the shrewd gaze of the same merchants who had observed Byron Wick and myself fifteen years before. Toby turned up wearing a white shirt and white pants — an ice-cream outfit — and the entire dining room turned and stared as we entered. He seemed to glisten with health and unscrupulousness. He held his face as if it were a coat-of-arms.

Toby was not one to fence with words. "Why you ask me to dinner, Michael?" He shrugged — a gesture too layered with meaning for me to decipher — and lifted his apéritif in his wide bony hand.

"I wanted to talk something over with you. About some research I'm doing."

Not true. I hadn't invited him here for that — at least I thought so. But the fact is, my destiny had not yet revealed to me that Toby's fate and mine were tied to that of Dedward and his female admirer.

And so I began to discuss my dilemma over a second round of drinks. Of course my hesitations, my scruples, were entirely lost on Toby. He was too simple, too selfish, for all that scholarly cavil. "So," I finished up, "I can't seem to make up my mind. Were they or weren't they? It's impossible to decide."

He looked at me, a little smile — flirtatious, condescending — on his lips. He seemed to enjoy my confusion. Then he shrugged. "Michael," he said, "let them to love each other." He shrugged again. He hadn't understood.

And then, quite suddenly, I wondered if he had understood better than I. At the same time I saw in his face a reflection of my old refusal. I had failed him, I had failed everyone. I had failed — it came to me in a spasm of pain — everyone but James Anthony Dedward.

"Love each other . . ." I echoed Toby's words, aware that the truth had been staring me in the face for weeks, months. *Dedward had never cared for Pallant Coombs — it had been his last, his greatest refusal.* And then I knew what I would do.

Toby was smiling broadly now, watching my face, sensing I had crossed some border to a country known only to myself. He reached over to pat my arm and I covered his hand with mine. He did not try to move it. "Yes," I breathed, my skin prickling, my ears roaring, "I will."

What can I say about the rest of that evening? I seemed to have changed into someone else entirely, as if another creature had been entombed in my body and now set free. After dinner Toby walked beside me—cutting through the misty night like a pirate sloop—to my apartment. Upstairs he didn't take a seat. Just moved around the living room, pacing, measuring, taking possession. He seemed very near and very distant at the same time and my earlier impression that I had crossed the border of a country quite new and strange intensified.

At last, at the door to the terrace, I put my hand on his back, feeling the firm skin under the white cotton. He turned his head and I kissed him. His lips were surprisingly soft. Then, without a word, we went into the bedroom. I had the odd notion that I had never entered it before.

That night, in my own bed, I enjoyed sex for the first time. Oh, I'd enjoyed it before—but not like this. I became a virtuoso of the bedchamber; I might have been invaded by a god. Now I know that if a god was present it was only Loki, god of mischief, but then it seemed I had never been so powerful, so possessed. Several times we stopped in our thrashing so that I might hold him against my lap. It was a move that nourished me profoundly, as if he were a baby or a Christ and I were his father or a Renaissance madonna. At the end, we seemed to have transcended the flesh entirely, bubbling higher and higher, our heads in the stars. Only at the last split second did I recall Bud Gorman. Later, laughing, exhausted, I understood that I had done it at last. Toby made me laugh again when he turned to me on the pillow and asked where I had learned all that. "From books," I replied.

The remark didn't interest him. He got up, his majestic organ almost unshriveled, and padded about looking for a cigarette. When he returned he was ready to talk about more practical things. He had an idea for importing Tunisian signet rings. Did I think I might help him with some financial backing? There was a killing to be made in the antiquities market.

Listening, my head resting on the small trampoline of his stomach, smoke enveloping us, I permitted myself a small ironic smile. Wasn't this exactly what I wanted? Wasn't it what I had admired him for, right along? A phrase of Céline's came to me, the description of a poor girl's physical charms: "her pocket gold mine." My head was very close to Toby's pocket gold mine. Could I blame him for wanting to make the most of it?

I agreed to put up some money for a sample shipment of rings. He would send some wires off tomorrow—to Tunis, to Paris. In his voice I heard the old casual arrogance. He had forgotten the last half-hour already.

And so my unmooring began. I pushed off from the familiar shore where I had lived all my life. Louisa was the first to notice. "You're becoming quite absentminded, Michael," she remarked as we crossed Waverly Place one afternoon. "I'd almost say rude if I didn't know you so well." I kept my mouth shut. How could Louisa understand, even if I could find the words to tell her? How odd it seems now, that with all my borrowed experience I didn't see that the events of my life could be fitted into old patterns, old traditions. Why didn't I try to explain myself to Louisa—who, after all, had shown herself to be a good friend? Now, looking back, I see that—believe it or not—I was simply too innocent to try. I was just a baby. I thought everything happening to me was happening for the first time in the history of the world.

I began to dress differently, exchanging my Irish knits and shapeless parkas for hip-huggers and tapestried vests and, around my neck, a medley of medallions and chains. I even bought boots with incurving heels—standard attire I had avoided in Denver—and teetered around Manhattan like a cowboy. Strangers, attracted or reassured by all this color, spoke to me easily, and I replied without shyness, as if we were all joined in some colossal joke.

Toby was delighted at the changes. He bought me a jacket with a buckskin fringe and insisted on my wearing it whenever we were together. Sometimes, when he examined me in my jacket, his eyes would glaze and his lips twitch and I knew he was fitting me into an American fantasy glimpsed once in Istanbul or on Corfu or Malta. At such times I would remind myself that no one, not even Toby, can live in a landscape that is not partly imaginary.

Once he took me to a penthouse party where rainbows of pills were passed around like canapés. I took two—the wrong two, apparently—because they canceled each other out and I woke up next day with nothing but a headache. At another party we wandered through a huge loft with serried columns like the Great Mosque in Córdoba, past futons placed end-to-end where men and women copulated amid piles of coats and scarves. After one of these affairs, as we walked back to my place, we couldn't stop laughing. We hooted and barked into the sinister night like schoolboys on holiday. The next day we stayed in bed, watching the shifting light on our bodies, exploring, feeding, coming down. I didn't even call the department secretary to cancel my classes.

People who knew me began to look at me suspiciously, even angrily. Maybe they thought I was acting irresponsibly. Maybe they thought I was imitating a Marxist history professor who had once barricaded himself behind the university computer and threatened to blow it up unless they enrolled more minorities. I don't know. I didn't care. I had left all that behind.

Underneath, other things were happening, events that would take me to the sixth floor at Misericordia. But then, when the administration people looked at me and tried to get past without speaking, I would boom out a greeting and insist on talking. That was the last thing they wanted—to be forced out of their disapproval, their fear. It was the conspiracy of the meek, who have inherited the earth before their time, and I was determined to fight it.

One hot night in July Toby and I found ourselves wandering toward the piers on the Hudson. The usual summer crowds were there. But this time they seemed, despite their macho masquerade, amazingly sweet and good-natured. It struck me that inside their leather and denim they were really quite mushy, unlike Toby who, inside his boutique clothes, was hard as steel. I was suddenly overpowered by the notion that they were all grown-up versions of Penrod, that monster of niceness, and that none of them had ever gotten access to the reek and danger of life. I looked at Toby as we walked. He was handsome and sleek as a Corsican bandit. I had had a narrow escape.

But I was not entirely free. Not yet. The thought, the possibility, that had inserted itself into my mind during our dinner at the Faculty Club, was still there. Waiting, unacted upon, unwritten. I could feel depression again, flapping its wings offstage. Suddenly, unaccountably, I went over to Toby—gazing at the filthy water over the railing—and pressed against him, hard. He let me do it for a moment, then disengaged, annoyed at such a naked expression of need. We were silent on the way home. At my door he excused himself, saying he wouldn't spend the night. It struck me he would wander off in search of better company—to Cory's perhaps.

I went upstairs thirsting for a drink, determined to find—or invent—a life I could live for good.

Dr. Gualtieri at Misericordia, whom I hated so much at first, told me in one of our early sessions that for some people breaking laws is as dangerous as breaking bones. He looked at me mildly after that, his blue eyes limpid behind wire frames, as if to establish our bond. The league of the just. It made me furious. I could feel the deadly net drawing around me again, choking and suffocating. He was amused and asked me to explain my anger. I couldn't—not then. Of course he knew nothing about literature. But I'm getting ahead of my story.

I had bought the ink—it was a dye, really, Luma's Hyacinth—almost in a dream, from an art-supply store on Canal Street. The nib pen came from a stationer's around the corner. They had sat, side by side, on my desk, for some time. Once in a while, hardly conscious, I practiced the spidery script on loose pages of paper. It was easy, right from the first, as if that feminine handwriting—the product of a young ladies' academy—had been encysted in my fingers for months, years, perhaps for my whole life. When the time was right, I would do it. In the meantime, I would practice.

A change, slight but significant, had come about in my relationship with Toby. He was—how shall I put it?—no longer in charge. He was no longer the teacher, I the student. We were partners now. Or perhaps, because I was senior by a dozen years, I dominated. At any rate, he watched me more carefully, listened more deferentially than before. When the first shipment of Tunisian rings arrived, and we had to make the rounds of the jewelers on 47th Street, he came tagging along like a boy. How I found the wit to outmaneuver those dark-eyed, beard-bedecked Hasidim, the triumphant survivors of a thousand years of pogrom, I don't know—but I argued, threatened, cajoled, and walked out until we got the prices we wanted. I told Toby it was up to him from now on—I was through—and he flinched at the thought of the battles ahead in that bazaar. But I knew he'd manage.

The invitation came in early September. School had just started, the trees in the park turning from their unhealthy green to a dull grey. It came in the form of a letter from the Victorian Society. The chairman of their program committee wanted me to address their annual conference at the Plaza. The theme was to be Dedward—that pillar of trans-Atlantic Victorianism. I was to choose any aspect of the life or work that interested me. I scribbled off an acceptance in the usual polite tones but my head was spinning with mischief. My chance had come at last. As I mailed off my reply I realized I was too excited to go home. I walked toward the river, aware that I had unlinked myself forever from my contemporaries, my compatriots. When I reached the Hudson, a sulphurous stream littered with garbage, I apostrophized them silently. "Goodbye," I whispered. "Goodbye."

When I got home I fixed myself a nightcap and took the little red journal from the metal box where I kept it. My hand was steady, my head clear. The violet sentences took shape smoothly and firmly — sentences scattered here and there, where space permitted. When I finished I riffled lightly through my emendations. A new element had been added to the last year of this lost lady's life. The pleasant notion occurred to me that she should be grateful. Hadn't I liberated her from her maidenly shroud? Hadn't I given her the lover she desired, the lover of her dreams?

Still, I was clever. My journal entries were understated, cryptic. Her style was mine; her abbreviations, her ellipses, her underscorings (and she was fond of underscoring), were mine. Everything that was to happen later — the quarrel with Dedward, the flight to Venice, the derangement and suicide — was adumbrated carefully. I knew my business, after all. It was a moment of truth toward which I had been tending for almost forty years.

I told Toby about it the next day. His eyes widened and deepened as he listened, then he smiled boyishly and kissed me. The kiss was a pledge, a contract. And, though I didn't know it at the time, a betrayal.

But I was free of my prison — and that was the most important thing. Free of the taffeta couch and the buried afternoons, free of my notes and books, free of the solitudinous life which had enclosed me in an embrace as cold, as vacant as that of James Anthony Dedward. By giving that wounded, incapacitated man a false love, I was free to claim my true one. I had become the outlaw of my dreams.

My speech at the Plaza caused a huge stir, of course. I became instantly notorious, at least in the little world of literary Victoriana. And there were echoes in the larger sphere — a mention in *Time* ("Dedward Expert Finds Papers Linking Author to Lady Novelist"), and a letter in the *New York Review of Books* (disputatious, of course). I remember my peroration quite clearly even now, given to a hushed room full of overstuffed figures who cried out for treatment by Cruikshank.

"Nature abhors a vacuum and the void at the center of Dedward's life has persisted too long. Now, at last, we may remove him from the list of those who never lived or loved, who never penetrated to the heart of the mystery, who never felt the claws of the beast as it sprang."

They crowded up to me afterward, hiding their jealousy behind tight scholarly smiles. But I fended off most of the queries. All in good time. Yes, my sources were impeccable. I would publish soon.

There was no serious challenge. Byron Wick's protégé was to be trusted. This was made even more clear when he made a statement from his home in Monterey, picked up by one of the wire services, to the effect that he had complete confidence in me.

Only Louisa Rosenquist permitted herself some skepticism. It was in a taxi going downtown after the conference, just the two of us. I caught glimpses of her under the street-lamps, her face harder and sterner than I had ever seen it—a Rhadamanthus come to judge the shades of the underworld.

"You wouldn't jeopardize your career for some silly personal reason?" Her voice was light and probing but underneath I heard unpleasant memories of my boozing, my irregular behavior, Toby.

"What kind of reason?" It was stupid to temporize with Louisa but I did it anyway.

"I don't know. Perhaps there's something you want to talk to me about, Michael."

The summons hung in the air like an echo from another life. But what was there to talk to Louisa about? It was all too late. In the next moment I wondered if what I had just done might not lead me to a solitude much greater than any I had known so far.

"Finding Pallant Coombs' journal is the kind of thing every scholar dreams about. Like the Boswell papers at Malahide Castle. And you want me to apologize." My tone was simple and grave, intended to deflect further questions. We didn't speak for the rest of the trip but when she got out she looked at me once—just once—and I knew I hadn't convinced her.

I waited as long as I could before taking the little journal to the librarian at Medford. It would be available only to certain scholars. The usual precautions. I riffled through it one last time, just before handing it over to Downes. There was no need to worry. Not even Pallant Coombs, returned to life, could have told her handwriting from mine. As for chemical analysis of the ink—if no one's suspicions were aroused, there would be no reason to request it. A far more likely reaction would be to claim that the lady wasn't telling the truth. Or that she was hysterical, describing a demon lover who had never been present in the flesh. Her tormented end would seem to favor such an interpretation. But I had my arguments ready for that too.

Within a week the little book had been handled by a dozen experts. Some had come with magnifying glasses. Another had gone to Conrad at the Argosy and asked to see the auction record. Another had cut a blank page from the back—quite unethically—for watermark dating. No one had thought to check the ink.

Within a month I knew I was safe. Nothing had reached my ears. The last, the greatest, the most Dedwardian hoax of all, had carried the day.

But I had overlooked one item—Toby Bellosguardo. The final paradox. The irony of ironies.

I don't recall exactly when Karen Tyler first came to the apartment. She'd been pursuing Toby for months, still coming up to him in Cory's, still inviting him to her table, her small face full of delight at the sight of him. I had never thought of her as a rival. Why should I?

The night Toby turned up with Karen in tow, I was actually glad to see her. They made a handsome pair. She was soft of voice, interested in everything. She seemed to know about some of our doings—a drive to Winterthur, the Tunisian signet rings. Toby invited her to stay for dinner. We were going to have a *choucroute garnie*.

They seemed very at ease with each other. I discovered that her father was a colonel in the Air Force and she'd grown up on bases overseas, including one in Turkey. Perhaps she had imbibed some of that same multinationality. They talked about diplomatic schools and legation parties and linguistic confusion and laughed a great deal. I had the feeling Toby was performing for her, putting on a show, as he had once done for me, and that he would soon return to the comfort, the routine, of our own relationship.

But once or twice, as the meal progressed, I read mischief in his eyes. Perhaps more than mischief—arrogance, coupled with that deadly charm of his. He drank more wine than usual, his face flushing, his accent thickening. But I didn't let anything upset me, not even when Karen, also a little drunk, sat in his lap and hung her honey hair over his face like a waterfall.

When he said he was going to see her home he threw me a look I had never seen before—anger mixed with defiance. It made no sense and I ignored it. He, like me, was entitled to his mischief.

He came back later, much later, stinking of her perfume. I woke up and decided not to interrogate him. It was none of my business really. He came to bed and went right to sleep, his heavy chest rising and falling, but my mind was overactive. I lay in the dark trying to put it all together. Toby might enjoy a triangle, with him at the center—or apex. It would feed his taste for intrigue, keep me off balance. I turned to look at him in the dimness. His profile might have graced a gallery in the Louvre. And then, despite—or because of—these new complications, a surge of delight went through me. Even a triangle was better than nothing—perhaps even better than a pairing. And then, pulling the sheet up to cover his shoulders, I understood that I had beaten my fate, the fate etched for me so long ago on a taffeta couch in Albany. I had averted the solitude, the fear. I had broken into that vacant house, my heart, and tenanted it with love, friendship, adventure. I had won. I had lived.

In the morning it was all over.

He had told Karen Tyler about the Pallant Coombs journal. Told it to her, a student, knowing exactly what she'd do. And she had. Gone to the department chairman, who'd gone straight to Louisa. She was on the phone to me before midday. A departmental meeting had been arranged—or rather a local inquisition. Louisa was wise enough not to ask me to explain anything in person. She simply asked me to stay away from school until the meeting. Just before hanging up she advised me that Byron Wick, summoned especially from California, would be in attendance.

There is very little to say about the nightmare of the next few weeks, especially since everything is a matter of record at Misericordia as well as in the files of the Sixth Police Precinct. I believe I could have faced it all, toughed it out, if Toby hadn't been involved. If he had been at my side instead of on the stand betraying me. But that, Dr. Gualtieri once said, was only the last flutter of my illusion. My relation with Toby, he claimed, was full of self-deception from the start. I never had the slightest idea what the boy was really like.

In any event, it was a hanging jury that awaited me in the conference room. Not only Louisa Rosenquist and Byron Wick (confined to a wheelchair) but others, less well-disposed, whom I had snubbed or frightened or patronized and were only too happy to see me brought low. Of course, I had thought of resigning beforehand, but it seemed unethical, more deeply unethical than anything I had done with Pallant Coombs' journal. I had had reasons for that, at least—reasons that made sense to me if not to my colleagues. But to have ducked out of this inquisition in advance would have been pure cowardice. Whatever my crime, cowardice had played no part in it.

Not that I was entirely sober when I walked through the door. Sobriety, under the circumstances, would have been asking too much. I had had enough to get me there, to keep me from breaking down as Toby, with his charmed smile, gave his testimony, and then to speak in my own defense.

My own defense. I wish I could say that I was Zola and Oscar Wilde and Socrates rolled into one. The truth is, my voice sounded slurred and feeble, even to me. But I tried. I spoke of my early attachment to Dedward and how he had freed me from the indignities of childhood. I spoke of the career that had been offered to me by Professor Wick and others. I spoke of the growing conviction that Dedward's refusals and my own were identical and that in order to free myself I must free him. At last I spoke of the ideology of the self and how two imaginary creatures may become fatally intertwined. But finally I trailed off. No one had understood. None of it made sense to them. I knew, from their downcast eyes and tight smiles, that my words had been too personal, too neurasthenic, too unscientific. They were shuffling their papers and thinking about revenge. It was then, when the room was silent, that Byron Wick, who had been so good to me, raised his withered arm in a gesture of impotent fury and said, "Michael, you have betrayed this department and this university, but worst of all, you have betrayed yourself. Yes, yourself." He broke down after that—perhaps it was senility—and had to be wheeled out. I remembered, with dreadful clarity, his retirement speech. He had spoken of the religion of art, the salvation of the word. I had believed all that once, with the fervor of an acolyte. How long ago it seemed.

Finally I was asked to leave. Silence surrounded me as I got up and wobbled toward the door. When I reached the outer room I too began to sob—dry shudders that produced no moisture. The secretaries refused to look at me.

It was the next morning that I found I couldn't tie my shoelaces. Strange, the things that trip you up in life. The laces wouldn't cross. Would . . . not. Such a simple thing, but no longer possible to my fingers. I sat on the bed for a long time, staring down. I wondered if the laces were the warp and weft of the world. I wondered if a pattern could no longer be woven on them. I thought other fancy thoughts. But the fact remained that there was no way under God's heaven I could tie my shoes and walk out the front door.

I tried to explain about the laces when they broke through the front door. The police, with Louisa close behind, were kindly but firm. They knew I was drunk—all the empty bottles proved that—but they weren't sure if I was crazy too. They decided to let the attendants on the sixth floor judge that.

And now I'm home again, alone, with only my memories, a few new friends, and this blue notebook. Toby came to see me once in the hospital but I was seized with such violent trembling that they had to send him away.

They took me very slowly along the track at Misericordia, the track grooved by so many misshapen imaginations before me. There were my daily sessions with Dr. Gualtieri, eternally wreathed in blue smoke. There was the group session, dominated by a tough dyke named Canta who never let me get away with any literary stuff. There were the evening meetings of the alcoholics—a sad, overhearty group with a tendency to spend time reminiscing about their most memorable highs. The hospital staff was very kind, as were some of my former colleagues from Medford, proving once again that, despite what you may have heard, all the world loves a loser.

Little by little I was brought back to life. It was a slow process; my imagination, after all, had been enslaved by a master. But toward the end of the fourth week, I realized that Dedward—the name is a bell tolling me to the grave—had had the last word all my life. In trying to escape him I had only proven his power over me. My progress was rapid after that.

And so I am home again. The place has been cleaned up, thanks to Louisa, and I can look back on the whole thing with some calm. There is no talk of reinstating me at Medford, but my therapist thinks they will come around in time, if I stay sober and if I want to teach again.

That's the last and toughest question. If I want to teach again. Part of me whispers I'd be better off in some other line of work. Another part of me points out that I have learned my lesson and can protect myself.

I haven'd decided yet. In the meantime I rest, write in this notebook and think about the fate that led me to literature at such an impressionable, such a corruptible age. A few days ago I passed Toby in the park. He peered at me curiously and tried one of his charmed smiles. Happily, I felt nothing. By the time I got home I was beginning to wonder if he had ever existed.

Other Grey Fox Books of Interest: